THE BONES OF NAPOLEON

THE BONES OF NAPOLEON

JAMES WARNER BELLAH

CUTTING EDGE

ISBN-13: 978-1-954840-59-1

Published by
Cutting Edge Books
PO Box 8212
Calabasas, CA 91372
www.cuttingedgebooks.com

CHAPTER ONE

THIS York Seat business began with a letter.

It was postmarked Baltimore, Maryland, four days before—October 12th, and addressed to M. L. Davanan, in care of Mr. Andrew Goldsboro, Attorney-at-Law, 24 Ferris Street, Baltimore. From the office of whoever Mr. Andrew Goldsboro might be, it had been readdressed to Mr. Davanan at 212 East 58th Street, New York City.

It was on the paper of the Baltimore Scrap Iron Company, 17 Water Street, Baltimore, Nathaniel Haugwitz, President, and it read:

DEAR MR. DAVANAN:

There is an old iron yacht at York Seat that has been there since about 1894.

If it is floatable, would you be open to an offer for it as scrap, subject to our survey?

Very truly yours,

N. HAUGWITZ

There were several reasons why Mat Davanan didn't answer it. In the first place, he had never heard of N. Haugwitz, Andrew Goldsboro, or the iron yacht, and not having heard of them he took it for granted that he was the wrong M. L. Davanan, put the letter back in its envelop, resealed it, marked it "opened by mistake" and sent it back to Baltimore.

Three days later he stopped at Tony's on the way home, and he stopped at the East New York Bicycle, Clam Bake, and Marching Club. And he stopped at Omaha Billy Martinelli's and he arrived at 212 East 58th Street in no condition to cope with the bones of Napoleon, which was what the second letter was about:

Mr. M. L. Davanan
212 East 58th Street
New York City
DEAR SIR:

I have been working for years on the latter phases of the life of Napoleon Bonaparte and the attempts made to rescue him from St. Helena and Elba, and I am absolutely certain as a result of my research that the last attempt was successful.

The rumor that he made his way to America has persisted for years but until recently I have given it no credence whatsoever. About a year ago, however, I came across a dossier of letters in the Bibliothéque Imperiale in Marseilles, the gift to the Library of the late Mrs. Henry Jerome of the Villa Croix de Cagnes, Cagnes-sur-mer, which support the rumor that Napoleon not only came to America but died there and is buried there—and not in Des Invalides.

The letters are from your ancestor, Robert Davanan, Esq. of York Seat, who died in 1835—to Marshal Bernadotte, who was then King Charles XIV of Sweden.

May I request you to let me have access to the library and records at York Seat at your convenience, and to forgive my inability to put a signature to this letter personally as it is impossible for me to hold a pen at present?

Most respectfully yours,

And in a fine slanting script—

INNES

And in the same fine script—

ANNE LANGDON

With typing below,

Secretary to Lord Innes

The St. Daviston Hotel
New York City
October 15th

Mat Davanan considered the letter solemnly as he lay down on his bed. He turned it upside down, sideways, diagonally. He looked at the signature closely.

"Anne," he said, "you write a beautiful hand. I'll bet you're a sight. A long beaked, flat-heeled horror."

Matthew Lloyd Davanan was twenty-eight—a tall, thin twenty-eight with red shot lightly through his hair and a fairly long, drawling horse-face below it. All good Amalgamated Press men look like that. He was in that period of development when the whole whirlpool of life centered on him—work, girls, hangovers, and a possible crack at fame. And because being the vortex was continually diverting, he gave none of it any very serious attention. He just lay quietly and let the breeze of its movement fan him—as he lay now on his couch in the noisome gunk hole he and Tom Powell referred to as home—and read Lord Innes' letter again.

Obviously there must be two M. L. Davanans, and he was still the wrong one. Outside, the traffic noises were softening and the October evening came down with the gentleness of a pleasant mood. And there was a knock on his door. He reached from the couch to the doorknob, turned it and looked up at the open doorway. A little man stood there with a brown felt hat on the back of his head. He was so knock-kneed that his heels were all of eight inches apart when his knees were together, but he had

3

magnificent shoulders that gave the lie to the weakness his legs implied. They seemed to move, those shoulders, even when he held them still as he was doing now, to move and swing downward from his neck to his thick arms.

"Somers, Missing Persons," he said and he pulled his right hand from his coat pocket and passed it, palm upward, under Mat's nose, as if he wanted him to smell it.

Mat said, "One step nearer the bed, Mr. Somers, and I take cyanide and smilingly I fall dead."

Somers said, "Are you Matthew Lloyd Davanan?"

Mat said: "Let's see the shield again." Somers poked it out once more. Mat took hold of his hand and held it under the bed lamp. It was a regular New York police shield all right—number 446,420.

Mat said, "That's my name."

Somers said, "What do you do?"

"City News, Amalgamated Press."

"That clicks. Where were you born?"

"Right here—in New York."

"That clicks. Father's name?"

"Murray Davanan. He's been dead twenty years."

"That clicks. Mother's name?"

"Margaret Vinson Davanan. She's been dead nine years."

"That clicks. Ever hear of a man named Charles Davanan?"

"Vaguely—just vaguely."

"What do you mean, vaguely?"

"I mean I hate his guts—I've never seen him—and I don't want to see him. He lives in Europe somewhere. He's my great-uncle."

"And you don't know him?"

"Why should I? I worked my way through college because he didn't know me. I never saw him in my life."

"But he's your great-uncle?"

"That's right. But don't hold it against me."

"I won't," Somers said. "Well, that's all I guess."

"The hell it is," Mat said. "What's this all about?"

"Just a check-up. The Baltimore police put in a request for it."

"What for?"

"How do I know?"

"Well, they can't just do that, can they?"

"They've done it, haven't they?" Somers said. "You ought to answer your letters. It would save the City dough," and he went out and closed the door.

Mat sat up on the couch and stared at the closed door. Now steady, he told himself—and watch the turns. And he got up and sloshed his face and hair down with cold water, combed his hair, and came back to the middle of the cluttered room. Tom Powell's bed was unmade still from the morning and the coffee-pot stood by the telephone at the head of it, with a cup stuffed full of butts. That meant Tommy had still been in bed when Mrs. O'Bannion cleaned up the place and made Mat's bed. There was a wad of Tom's clothes on the floor in front of the closet. That meant Tom had gotten up and dressed after Mrs. O'Bannion had finished her chores and left.

Mat looked it all over. Now look—this is where you are and this is where you stay. Don't get your hopes up. The Baltimore police may be looking for an M. L. Davanan and the Baltimore Scrap Iron Company may want to buy an old hull from M. L. Davanan—but none of it's got anything to do with you. If your Uncle Charles is dead—you won't get a dime. Your grandfather left Baltimore years ago. Your old man hated that branch of the family, your mother always thought they were hot-house orchids. This Charles Davanan married a rich English Jewess—banks or something, and there it ends. Whoever they want isn't you—and whatever they want them for—you won't get. Go to bed .... And he went to bed.

The alarm bonged. Nine A.M. He reached for the telephone and dialed City News. "B.K.? Davanan. What's on the board? I'm at 59th and Fifth."

"The hell you are. You're in bed. Get up and get down to the Criminal Courts Building."

Mat hung up. Tommy Powell hadn't come in all night—which was all right, Tom being a man of regular habits, too. He set the alarm for ten and folded up again. It bonged ten.

With that he got up and shaved. He boiled coffee. He dressed. He smoked and there was a knock at his door. A woman.

"I'm Mrs. Vom Bloercke," she said. "I'm looking for Mr. Davanan. The cleaning woman downstairs said that this was his door. Are you he?" In spite of her name she was an American and she was a lady—and she was quite shockingly beautiful. That is, she was excessively beautiful and it was shocking to see that beauty going under the fire of some inner turmoil that she held tightly to her soul lest it flame and consume her. Immaculate. That is something so intangible in women, the quality of fine detail, a breath of completion, the spirituality of line drawing. Mat stared at her and it flashed through his mind suddenly that she was not there at all—that in a moment he would see the wall beyond—through her.

A nerve chill ran down his arms to his elbows and for a moment he was completely unhorsed. This, in New York City in broad daylight. She was exquisitely dressed and completely there as a woman before him—all but her eyes. That was what did it—her eyes. They were a pale, washed blue—but there was absolutely nothing in them. The fire of them had gone out. It was horrid, seeing that.

He said: "Won't you come in, Mrs. Vom Bloercke," and he was terribly embarrassed as he said it. She seemed to pick that up, for she smiled.

He said: "I am M. L. Davanan," and he held the door wide for her. The whole thing was *fey* now. He had the New York habit of looking all women over quickly for what they were, what they had and what they offered—but that wasn't in this at all. This was some quick compulsion to help—to hold out a sustaining hand to—to listen to with charity, if you will. She stepped into the room and he said, "There is a chair somewhere—here," and he pulled it out for her.

She smiled again and sat down crossing her gloved hands one over the other on her crossed knee. He stood in front of her, helpless for a second, then he said, "Cigarette?" He shoved his box toward her.

"No," she shook her head. "You know me, don't you?"

"Yes," he said solemnly. "In a very peculiar way I do know you. I know I've never met you or seen you before but it seems that I do know you. Screwball?"

She smiled, "I didn't know it before I came into this room, but I know you, too."

"Do you?" he watched her eyes steadily.

"Yes," she said. "Sir Henry Raeburn painted you in 1809. You are Captain the Honorable Eric Molleston, Royal Navy. You hang in the Tate Galleries in London. A lady died for you once."

Matthew laughed. "I'm sure that's not possible," he said. "I was in prep school in 1809."

She leaned toward him and the gesture was as compelling as if she had reached out and touched him. A definite gesture that held him where he was and held him silent—a dramatic compulsion, if you will, to which there was no calling to, no stopping—nothing but quiet acquiescence. And in that moment he knew that it would be impossible for him to refuse her wishes or to disregard her commands. His fingers were numb with the feeling, his breathing tight—but he broke it suddenly—broke it through sheer masculine bludgeoning.

"What lady died for me?"

Mrs. Vom Bloercke pulled herself up—pulled herself up physically until she sat there in front of him, every muscle in her body drawn so tight that they almost sang with the tension. A woman who had been terribly hurt by life—protecting herself instinctively from all future wounds.

"Her name," she said, "was Madeleine Bligh," and she closed her eyes tightly and touched them briefly with the finger tips of her left hand.

Mat didn't know what he had now. He was stopped, dead back on his heels. Whatever it was that was passing in the woman's mind was of desperate emotional importance to her and he dare not, for the moment, interrupt it.

She moved her hand and opened her eyes. She said, "It is strange that we should think we knew each other, but it can't be anything but coincidence, you see. Mr. Davanan—I want to rent York Seat for three months."

He opened his mouth.

"Your house," she said.

"I'm terribly sorry—" he shook his head, "I—"

She raised her hand. "No—please—hear me out first. It may seem odd to you if I describe myself quite frankly as a mental patient. Quite a harmless one, I assure you. I manage all my own affairs and I have no attendants, nor have I ever been confined. But I live entirely in the past—not actually, you understand, but in my inner life. I don't see things or have hallucinations of any kind—but in some intangible way all my spiritual being flamed to its vital heat a century ago—there I began and there I ended—"

Matthew reached for a cigarette and ran it through his fingers. "Go on."

"—at York Seat," she said. "I want to rent it from you. I want to go there and live for a while—quite alone. I am not a wealthy woman, but I'm prepared to offer you five hundred dollars a month for it for three months, with an option of three months longer—"

"My dear Mrs. Vom Bloercke—I don't own a house! I'm a very mediocre newspaper man. I've got three suits of clothes and I share this walk-up with a friend who pays all the rent at present because I play the ponies. There I begin and there I end."

"But that can't be," she smiled, "for you are Matthew Lloyd Davanan."

He shook his head and smiled. "You're wrong, too," he said quietly. "That is the place Charles Davanan owned. Apparently he is dead—"

"He is dead—he died ten days ago."

"He did?"

"Yes—that's why I've come to see you."

"But I haven't anything to do with it."

"It's been left to you."

"No. That wouldn't be possible," Mat said. "You see that branch of the family and my branch have been estranged for three generations."

"But your lawyer in Baltimore—Mr. Goldsboro—"

"Mrs. Vom Bloercke—I haven't any lawyer in Baltimore—"

She stood up very slowly, an infinite sadness in her eyes.

"No—no—please!" he held out his hand. "Let's get this straight."

"I told you—about me," she said with some dignity, "because I am not ashamed of myself or the condition of my mind. I told you the truth because I thought you would understand it—but it doesn't always pay." She opened her handbag and took out a silver card-case. She slipped three cards from it. "This," she said, "is my bank in New York. The Grand Central Branch. Mr. Graffon, the President, will vouch for me financially. "This," she said, is my attorney. Mr. Upjohn of Stone, Satterlee, Upjohn and Faynes. And my doctor happens to be in town also. Dr. Gabor de Wolff. He will tell you what else you require to know."

"But I tell you—I don't own a house—much less York Seat."

"Please rent it to me—" she smiled sadly. *"Please."*

"My dear lady—if I owned it I would. I—"

"Please," she handed him the cards and crossed to his door. "I need a few months there alone—so badly."

"Don't go." He followed her to the door and put his hand out to her. She turned and smiled sadly.

"You see," he said, "I really don't own York Seat yet—and I really don't know anything about my owning it ultimately—it isn't what you have told me about yourself. Why should it be?"

"Thank you," she nodded slightly. "You are terribly kind."

"No," he shook his head, "not as a general rule—but there is something about you that makes me want to be kind to you—makes me want to help you. Does that seem absurd to you?"

"No."

He said, "If I did own this York Seat—I'm quite sure I should let you go down there for as long as you wanted to go—as my guest—without asking you why you wanted to go."

She closed her eyes tightly for a moment.

"But that would be very rash of you," she said, "wouldn't it?"

"Perhaps—but I should do it."

"And yet I might be the cheapest of crooks."

"Yes—you might be, but you aren't, you see. You are a very charming person in very desperate trouble. You would be that—and you would be quite honest to me without your bank, your lawyer, and your doctor to give you characters."

"And you wouldn't even ask why I wanted to go to York Seat?"

He laughed. "Yes—I'd have to. I have to now. Not for what you might do there, but to satisfy my own curiosity. Why is it so necessary for you to go there?"

She sat down again and looked at him for a long moment. "I would much prefer my doctor to explain it to you, for I am too deeply in it as a patient to do the intricacies of it justice."

"Try," he said.

She looked at the palm of her gloved hand. "York Seat," she said, "represents the greatest tragedy of my dream life. How that particular place in all the world happens to be my focal point, I can not tell you, but it does. And it is on it, that my unwinding, my cure, if I am to be cured, must be based."

"No," he smiled, "by me."

"I was afraid it would be," she said, "but it is as simple as this. A year ago I found myself in New York on the eve of sailing. I was under treatment then, with Dr. de Wolff. On the way to the liner, I knew I couldn't go—I knew that I had to hire a car and drive southward. My doctor insisted I do it. He came with me. We started at once. I drove the complete distance from Grand Central to York Seat, without knowing where I was going, without a road map, help, or directions of any kind. At the gates, I fainted. For a time Dr. de Wolff discounted the whole thing. He brought me back to New York and hospitalized me for a month. Then I did go to Europe. But York Seat remained a part of me. Finally de Wolff accepted it. He has unwound my spool to it and he now wants me to go there and do the rest of the work myself."

Mat stood up. "It's fairly clear now," he said. "And quite logical as you say it."

"I'm glad," she held her hands half out toward him. He wanted to reach for them and take them in both of his, but he couldn't. He wanted to kneel before her and tell her just what it was that she was doing to him—that by just being there with him, she was taking all that he was from him and leaving him helplessly behind. And then suddenly he was frightened with race memory or what you will. This is that one dread thing with a woman that steals your mind and your happiness forevermore. This urge to serve to the complete destruction of self. Once you have given a woman that—your manhood is gone in the selflessness of love—and you are a lost soul whether she reciprocates or not, for you have been untrue to the instinct to dominate and you have granted her masculinity for finding the Achilles heel of femininity in you. He must take her quickly now—or run from her. There could never be a middle course with her. Pick her up in his arms and carry her to his bed—or turn from her and run headlong down the stairs and leave her.

She saw it all in his eyes. She stood up, very straight before him. "Of course," she nodded, "that must be a part of us. I have known it, since I came into this room and saw you. But not here—and not now. Beautifully, Matthew—and somewhere—in our time." And she went out.

The door closed and Mat stood for a moment unable to move, with the insane feeling that none of it had happened. But the breath of her perfume was in his nostrils still and the memory of her was in his blood.

He looked stupidly at the cards. Underneath her name on one she had written "Mr. Herbert Graffon, Mo. 9-7723," her banker. On the second, "Mr. Ralph Sturdevant Upjohn, Jo. 3-2266," her lawyer. And on the last "Gabor de Wolff, M.D., Pl. 7-1740."

The cards were her own, beautifully engraved—

MADELEINE BLIGH VOM BLOERCKE

CHAPTER TWO

MAT couldn't think in the Balkan air of the subway so he got out at Fourteenth Street, walked over to Fifth and climbed up on top of a bus.

It's fantastically impossible that I've inherited York Seat—or I'd have heard. Besides—I wouldn't possibly come into it. They cut Father's old man off with a trust fund for a gold-brick deal he pulled on his friends in Baltimore years ago—and for marrying his boarding-house-keeper's daughter on top of it. I suppose they knew about Father—but how the hell would they know about me? Mother hated the Maryland tribe—and talked them down for social phonies. We never have had any contact with them. Why would they look me up, three generations later to leave me a house? In England, yes—but not in this country. Those things don't happen.

He got off at the Library and went up to the third floor to the card index, and after a few minutes of pawing through it he handed in a chit for *Eastern Shore Manor Houses,* and sat down to it.

It was one of those heavy romantic drools, that book, that certain types of well-born patriotic spinsters will write. And nothing can be done about it. The spinsters are usually named Smith or Jones or Haney, but their mothers were Randolph's, by God, which is probably why democracy is dying:

York Seat, the ancestral home of the Davanan Family stands on the slightly rising ground above the Bligh River, about three quarters of a mile from Wreck Point on the Little Creek Road. It is a Georgian Mansion, much on the same architectural lines as Doughoregan Manor, in a complete state of preservation, and still owned by the descendants of Robert Davanan, Esquire, to whom Lord Baltimore gave the original grant of thirty thousand acres. Not as large as Wye House, the ancient seat of the Lloyd Family in Talbot County, York Seat is, however, more modernized, for the present owner, Mr. Charles Davanan, at one time spent a considerable amount of money on improvements and restoration and in dredging the Bligh River.

Bligh again—and with the name in print, that elusive perfume of Mrs. Vom Bloercke came back to him:

...the British Fleet took four hundred slaves from York Seat and all the silver, a few days before it burned Washington in 1813. Robert E. Lee used to visit there when he was a cadet at West Point, and it is said that he once scratched his initials on one of the windows with the diamond in some young lady's engagement ring. Thomas Jefferson is said to have drawn the plans for the orangery on the back of an envelop once, when Colonel Matthew Davanan was visiting him at Monticello after the Revolution. Admiral Badenoch lies in the family burial ground as does the body of that tragic English gallant, Captain the Honorable Eric Molleston, R. N., who was killed in a duel at York Seat in 1809....

Mat tore back to the card index and checked out Malinoff's *Sir Henry Raeburn*—the edition with color plates. In the index to plates, Molleston's portrait was listed—page 279 with the notation, Tate Gallery. He turned to page 279.

The face that stared up at him was fat. The face of a man fat in body and fat in mind. It wore the traditional Royal Navy beard but it wore it so consciously combed and trimmed to fit, that there was the instinctive feeling that it was there to hide a miserably weak mouth and chin. Raeburn didn't like Captain Molleston. Mat didn't like him. What in hell resemblance the portrait bore to him with his long horse-face and his red hair he was frankly damned if he knew. How Mrs. Vom Bloercke could possibly see any similarity was beyond him.

"Will you be long with that book?"

Mat looked up. A girl was standing to his right, slightly behind his chair, looking down at him. Self-contained, with the intangible breath of cool decency about her which is rare in young women in New York. A slender girl with a certain defi- nite stamina. A soft tweed skirt, a tweed cape and a brown hat of expensive felt—all of it a delicate line that showed intelligent female thought about the matter. Twenty-four perhaps—not much more. And definitely good-looking. Her eyes did it first— the clean line of her nose, the honesty of her full mouth.

He picked up *Eastern Shore Manor Houses.* "This book?" he asked her.

"Yes," she said.

"Well, I don't know," he said solemnly. "You see I stutter ter- ribly and I have been going to a school to correct it. They sent me over here to memorize this book from cover to cover so that I can recite it—"

"But this isn't possible—" she reached suddenly to the table for the slip he had signed. "Are you Mr. Davanan?"

"I am," he said.

She pulled up the next chair and sat down, smiling. "I've just come from your apartment. You've got a most amusing friend."

"You want to be very careful of him," Mat said. "His name isn't Tom Powell at all. It's Baby Face Collins. He's got a touch of the tarbrush and he's wanted for trunk murders in four states. He has spells, too—he hits girls with meat axes. I wouldn't have much to do with Tom Powell," he shook his head, "if I were you."

"I'm Anne Langdon," she smiled. "Lord Innes' secretary. I wrote you a letter a couple of days ago—"

"There really is a Lord Innes then?"

"Of course there is. He's a dear old soul. He's written twenty books and he is Chairman of the Board of the Irish National Museum. He's writing a book now on Napoleon and he wants to go down to your house in Maryland and work in the library there—on the old records. He's out of bed to-day and he's impatient—that's why I went to your apartment to see if you got the letter."

"Look," Mat said. "I'm a simple soul at heart and I work for a living—and this whole thing is coming at me so fast I can't duck. I don't own a house in Maryland to start with. And right after that a Mr. Haugwitz wants to buy a yacht, you want the bones of Napoleon, a detective gets after me to see if I'm me and a Mrs. Vom Bloercke died for me a hundred and thirty years ago when I wore a beard. What would you do under the circumstances—draw cards?"

"But you do own the house!" the girl said, "if you're Matthew Davanan."

"Well, if I do—it's being kept from me and I resent it," he grinned, "bitterly."

"But Mr. Goldsboro told us you owned it—he referred us to you! We arrived in New York ten days ago, Lord Innes and I, and we went directly to Baltimore expecting to go on over to the Eastern Shore, but we arrived in Baltimore two days after Mr. Goldsboro got word of Mr. Davanan's death at York Seat."

"Go on."

"That's all," Anne said, "except that Mr. Davanan's will left York Seat to you as the only surviving member of the family. Andrew Goldsboro wrote you about it, asking you to come to Baltimore at your convenience, and he suggested we wait for your permission."

"But I've had no letter from Andrew Goldsboro."

"That's strange. He looked up your address in the New York telephone book—212 East 58th Street, for he gave it to me and he said that he had forwarded mail to you there and referred several inquiries to you."

"I guess he had all right—I've had plenty—all but his."

Anne said, "Lord Innes and I came directly back to New York to see you, and Lord Innes was taken ill and has been ill in bed ever since we got here. So I wrote you a letter—which you haven't answered either."

Mat Davanan sat back in his chair.

"Well," she laughed, "does Lord Innes get to work in the library?"

The dark little man across the table from them got up suddenly and said, "For gossakes, does any one get to work in any library?" and he walked off.

"Talkative fellow," Mat said. "Lord Innes certainly does get to work in the library—if the house is mine. I wouldn't be without any of you. You, Lord Innes, Mrs. Vom Bloercke, the Baltimore Scrap Iron Company and the bones of Napoleon. Now about your personal habits. Do you drink cocktails with strange young men? And if you do, how many do you drink and what time of day do you start?"

She said, "I work for a living. I'm here to get the list this book gives of the people buried in the York Seat graveyard—and I've got to go right back to the St. Daviston when I'm through."

"I'll take you back. Here—get started on the book."

He watched her closely as she ran through the tomb list, taking the names down on her pad in shorthand. A nice job of girl, Anne Langdon. Easy—with none of that coy guile the darlings spread their nets with. This girl was an open-face model, cool, clean, and pleasant. It would take a hell of a lot to wring tears out of her. And two-timing wasn't in her for one-timing wasn't, if you follow Mat's mind. She wasn't asking anything from any man yet, for she had what she wanted herself—a job, work, independence, and an eye for quiet amusement.

When she finished writing, he said:

"What do you do, just knock around the world working for the Peerage?"

"For a year I have," she said. "My father left me enough to start out with—so I went to London tourist and put an ad in the paper and pulled Lord Innes out of the hat first try."

"Good girl."

Lucky girl," she smiled. "I've always been lucky. That was the bulk of the estate my father left me—his luck. Priceless luck."

They got up and started out and down the marble stairs to the Fifth Avenue entrance.

"What was he, a bookmaker?"

"My father?" she laughed. "He was a painter."

"What kind of a painter?"

"How he would have loved that question!"

"Wrong again?"

"No," she shook her head. "Simply that he will some day be known as the greatest painter of his time—in America."

"Really?"

"The Metropolitan bought two of his canvases while he was still alive. He was in Who's Who in Art before he was thirty," she said. "I think he was the greatest American painter since George Bellows."

He raised his finger for a cab and handed her in. They sat for a moment as the cab turned, not touching shoulders, not speaking.

She looked at him intently. He was rather long in the nose and the cheek-bones, but decidedly pleasant around the eyes and there was an earnestness in him suddenly that was definitely compelling. His hand on her arm had been warm and capable and the easy lines of the man were whip-strong. For the first time in her life, she felt a complete confidence in some one she didn't know and for one awful moment she wanted him to reach for her and hold her tightly in his arms, put his hands on her and give her strength. And that frightened her for she saw in his eyes, the brief shadow of feeling that clouded her own. Those things happen quickly like mist in stream hollows. One moment the air is clear, and the next the thin skein of instinct is there, weaving through it, coiling, tightening.

"Well?" he said softly. "There it is, isn't it?" And he pulled her gently toward him. She reached out for him and he caught her in his arms and for a brief second they looked into each other's eyes and saw all that there ever is to see. Then he kissed her gravely and the taxi faded and for a flash, they were one person, complete and invincible—but a brief flash, for they both pulled back at once, startled at their own intensity—frightened.

"That," she said quietly, "—is that, isn't it?"

"Yes," he nodded.

And they sat there, looking at each other, not understanding quite how this thing had happened to them, but knowing definitely that it had been the most logical thing in the world.

"Do you take chances like that often?" she asked him.

"Was it a chance?" he said. "It didn't seem like one somehow."

"It was," she nodded, "for you. You see, I know everything there is to know about you—but you know absolutely nothing about me. I may be leading you on into something that you may regret. It is very careless of you to kiss strange young women."

"I suppose you are right," he grinned, "in theory. But in this specific case you wanted me to kiss you and I wanted to kiss you. So we did. And that happens to be that."

She looked down at her hands. "Yes," she said. And amazingly, the cab had pulled up under the crystal canopy of the Hotel St. Daviston.

"Now what do we do?" Mat asked her.

"Well, it won't do for you to barge in on Lord Innes now," Anne told him. "You must write him or telephone him first. He's a very meticulous old fellow and he doesn't understand informality. Besides, he's undoubtedly working now. Suppose you drop me here and telephone him early this evening."

"And what about you?"

"I shall answer the telephone," she smiled.

He looked at her for a moment. "You're the pleasantest thing that's happened to me in years," he said slowly.

The color rose in her cheeks.

"I'm really a very improper young woman," she said. "I assure you I kiss every man I meet—exactly as I kissed you—it's something I can't help."

He laughed. "So do I, you liar," and he got out and let her go.

CHAPTER THREE

L ATE that afternoon when he got the sign-off from B.K. he ran into Tommy Powell at the apartment as he did now and then.

"You must excuse my not dropping in last night," Tommy said, "but a strange thing happened. A very old friend of mine arrived in town—and we went to the Aquarium."

Tommy was a small cheerful hedonist with curly blond hair all over his head and the stout, chubby body of a successful glutton. He said: "How about a girl named Anne Langdon—a rather tidy bit of girl, I should say, who definitely needs a guiding masculine hand in her life? What about such a girl, Matthew? Give out."

"You saw her," Mat said. "To-day. Here. For the last time. I see her from now on."

"Oh, come, come," Tommy said. "My interest is purely academic in these matters, as you well know. But the point is with this Anne Langdon, I seem to place the numero somewhere in the dim past but I can't quite get her in focus."

"What do you mean you place her?"

"Just that," Tom said. "I've seen her before. There's some story behind her I can't quite get."

"No sale with this girl. She's only been in this country ten days after a year in England."

"Nope," Tommy shook his head. "I can't be wrong. Not Eagle-eye Powell. That girl's been in the public prints. There's something about her. I'll get it."

"You're crazy. She's only a kid."

"Yes, yes, my boy. Yes, yes. But I'll get it."

"Her father was a painter. The Met. bought some of his stuff and he was in Who's Who in Art before he was thirty."

"Nope," Tommy said, "something else—something prime—something juicy. I'll get it. Don't you worry. I'll get it. There are two special delivery letters for you and an Eton and Oxford and veddy good Regiment gent, Gabor de Wolff called you on the telephone. I told him you'd be in around this time—perhaps sober."

Mat crossed to the desk and picked up the two letters. From Sloan, Satterlee, Upjohn and Faynes, 40 Wall Street, this:

DEAR SIR:

A former client of mine who wishes to rent some property from you, Mrs. Madeleine Bligh Vom Bloercke, desires me to write to you and to satisfy you in the matter of her personal references.

She is a lady of impeccable antecedents who, I am sure, will make you a satisfactory tenant in every respect. Any further information that I can give you, I shall be glad to furnish.

Very truly yours,

RALPH STURDEVANT UPJOHN

And from the Seaforth National Bank, Grand Central Branch, Office of the President, this:

DEAR MR. DAVANAN:

One of our depositors, Mrs. Madeleine Vom Bloercke, desires me to write to you to inform you that you may refer to us for her financial integrity in the matter of the property she desires to rent from you.

Yours very truly,

HERBERT GRAFFON, *President*

Mat said, "Thomas—don't look too quickly, but I think I've struck gold," and he told him about York Seat.

Tommy said, "It sounds all right from here—but mind your pipe doesn't go out."

Mat said: "My luck will work it out like this. I'll get York Seat for free—but no dough with it. I can sell that old yacht that's on the place for about eighteen dollars to the Baltimore Scrap Iron Company—and rent the place to Mrs. Vom Bloercke for fifteen hundred dollars. With that—and two years of my salary, I can meet the tax bill for this year. You watch. I'm like that."

Tommy said, "That would be the downstairs bell," and he went through, punched the buzzer and opened the hall door. They heard the street door clunk shut below and footsteps on the stairs.

That was Dr. de Wolff.

Gabor de Wolff was a tall man with a touch of the Guardee in mufti. His tailoring punched him out in silhouette with long, decisive lines. Spiritually, he wore white linen spats and a carnation and carried a Briggs umbrella neatly furled. Spiritually, he was a heel clicker at introductions—a precise bower-from-the-waist. Actually, he did none of those things, but the promise of all of them was there, like hidden blued-steel springs under his casual smartness. His hair was black and polished down tightly to his round, military head. His hands were long and narrow and exceedingly strong. His legs were slender, hunting-boot legs. He moved with the full, controlled speed of a healthy animal, but his eyes were not healthy. They were smeared black with shadow under his black brows and shone through the shadow with a metallic gleam. When they moved, they clicked almost audibly. He approached people and enveloped them with his ease and fine manners, folded himself completely around them and compelled them in the thin liquid cement of his personality.

"Ah, yes, Mr. Davanan. I'm Dr. de Wolff. I called you to-day."

"Yes."

"And I found myself in the neighborhood, so I have dropped in on Mrs. Vom Bloercke's behalf, for I'm leaving in a day or so for Europe." His voice was meticulous, excellently rounded English spoken with a mechanical precision that made Mat wait for the rhythm to complete itself before he broke in on it.

"I suppose I should have called you," Mat said. "She left me your number. Her bank and her lawyer have already written to me."

"Yes," de Wolff nodded. "A strange case," he put his hands together in his lap.

Mat nodded.

"I can assure you," de Wolff said, "that in the common acceptance of the term, she is not insane. That is why I am here. I happen to be her psychoanalyst."

One of those boys, Mat thought. That's what gives him the eyes.

"Part of the results of her self-treatment is her frankness, Mr. Davanan."

"I see."

De Wolff said: "I don't know how much you know about the mind, but undoubtedly you know that the potentialities of no two minds in this world are identical. Therefore the use of the word 'normal' can never be applied because there is no norm except in mass behaviorism. There being no definite norm, then there can be no point of demarcation between normality and abnormality except in the same terms of mass behaviorism. I can assure you," he smiled, "that Mrs. Vom Bloercke is not insane.

"Her life has been tragic and she has withdrawn slightly from it, to escape that tragedy. She has mildly associated her own life with the life of a Madeleine Bligh who lived a century ago. She doesn't actually believe she is the reincarnation of that other Madeleine Bligh—but the similarity of her life and that other woman's life has intrigued her. I have Mrs. Vom Bloercke's spool unwound that far. Now I want her to live in the milieu that other

Madeleine Bligh lived in—so she can rewind the spool herself. I want her to live at York Seat—the place in Maryland that she wants to rent from you."

"I get it. It's damned interesting."

"Yes," de Wolff nodded. "I think so."

"I see," Mat said.

"Then may I tell her—and will you have the lease drawn up?"

Mat said: "No—not as fast as that, I'm afraid. I haven't been notified yet that I've inherited the place. I don't think there is much doubt that I have—"

"You have—I can assure you. Mrs. Vom Bloercke is a most meticulous woman in all her affairs. She saw your great-uncle's lawyer in Baltimore, a Mr. Andrew Goldsboro."

"But Mr. Goldsboro hasn't been in touch with me yet. Nothing has been done. I haven't been notified—or if I have, I haven't received the letter. There's been no transfer of the property."

"Oh—I see—well, in that case—until it is settled finally, I suppose we can do nothing."

"Naturally not—"

"But I may tell Mrs. Vom Bloercke that when it is settled—that you will rent the place to her?"

"Does she know what kind of a house it is? Frankly, I don't—except that it hasn't been lived in for forty years. The bathrooms, if there are any, must be fairly sketchy—all that."

"I don't think that will matter. She is a woman of some means. She will probably make a part of the house liveable, she plans to bring servants and furniture."

"Wait a minute—there's another thing," Mat said suddenly. "There's an old man in town who wants to do some research work in the library at York Seat. I've just told his secretary that he may do it."

Dr. de Wolff sat back in his chair, looking steadily at Mat. He said, after a moment: "Mrs. Vom Bloercke wanted to be there alone—except for her servants."

"Suppose we let it all go until I hear definitely. Then we can work it out."

"Time with Mrs. Vom Bloercke's treatment is an element," de Wolff said. "Who is this man who wants to work in the library?"

"Lord Innes. He's ill at the Hotel St. Daviston."

"I see. Well—" de Wolff put his hands gently on his knees and stood up. "I'm glad I talked to you, Mr. Davanan. It was my duty to Mrs. Vom Bloercke, I felt."

"Naturally."

"Shall you go to York Seat?"

"I expect so, as soon as I know. I've never seen the place."

"But that won't be for a few days anyway. A week or two, let's say?"

"I would say so."

"And what may I tell Mrs. Vom Bloercke?"

Mat said: "I feel rather sorry for her—she seems to have had a lot of trouble. Tell her to give me a week or so to straighten this thing out—to go down and look the place over. Perhaps Lord Innes can finish his work there in that time—and when all the details are straight, she can have it for three months—at her figure."

When he left them, Tommy said: "That fellow's got something. I don't know what it is but he puts it over. You believe him. You want to like him and you want him to like you."

Mat took a shower and changed, and when Tommy went out on his date he called the St. Daviston and asked for Lord Innes' secretary. In a moment he had Anne Langdon's full-throated voice on the other end.

"Dinner?" he said. "This is the man about the girl who knocks around the world working for the Peerage."

She laughed. "I've had dinner," she said.

"Who was the man?"

"No man, just me alone with a tray. I'm still working."

"All right—how late are you going to keep it up?"

"Until midnight."

"That's rather final for to-night then, isn't it?"

"I'm afraid so," she said.

"What time to-morrow?"

"Lunch—if you come. I've just mailed a letter to you, asking you—or rather for Lord Innes asking you. Will you wait a minute—the telephone is ringing in the living-room." She put down her instrument. After a few moments she came back and picked it up again.

"Well?" he said.

"It was another man," she said.

"For you—or the old boy?"

"For Lord Innes," she said, "but he disconnected."

"What are you on—twenty-four-hour duty?"

She laughed. "No—but I take care of the telephone when it rings. Lord Innes is in bed."

"You must have quite a plant there."

"His room," she said, "the living-room—and mine."

"It sounds very cosy for forty dollars a day."

"Have you heard about York Seat yet?"

"No," he said.

She said: "Wait a minute—there's some one knocking at the door now," and she put the telephone down again. He waited—but she didn't come back to the phone. Presently he began to watch the hand of his wrist-watch. Three minutes, four, five. He disconnected and rang the hotel again.

"Lord Innes' secretary."

"Her line is busy, I'm sorry."

"I know—I was on it. I disconnected my end by mistake."

"Well, I can't connect you again until she hangs up."

He lay back and reached for a cigarette, and in about five minutes he called her again. He got her this time.

Her voice was strained. "Can you call back later," she asked quickly, "—or to-morrow?"

"Why—what's up?"

"An awful thing—we've just been broken in on."

"How?"

"The place is full of house detectives—I can't talk."

"Tell me—or I'll come over and break in on you myself. Are you hurt?"

"Of course I'm not hurt—I'm terrified. It must have been the man who telephoned. He must have done that to see if we were in. He knocked on the door of the living-room and stuck a gun in my ribs. He turned out the lights before I could really see him and made me lead the way to Lord Innes' bedroom. He turned out the lights in the bedroom and stood at the foot of the bed. He said, 'Not this time. I'm warning you, Sir!' And poor Lord Innes said, 'I do not know you, Sir!' And that was all. He went out as he had come in and we put on the lights and called the desk. They've notified the police."

"But it doesn't make sense—did he take anything?"

"I can't talk any more," she said quickly. "The old man is terribly upset and the police have just arrived—to-morrow..." and she clicked off.

CHAPTER FOUR

H E stared at the telephone for a moment, then he grabbed his hat and started for the door. No—steady. You can't go over there and barge in, cold turkey. He walked back to the center of the room and lit another cigarette. He pushed the table away from the window and stood there looking down into 58th Street. The girl, he said, has got you. As simple as that. You go along meeting them for years casually—and then one of them steps out of the crowd—and she's yours. You know it as soon as she smiles—as soon as you see her eyes—feel the soft warmth of her hand on yours. "Did he hurt you?"—as simple as that, for that's all that matters.

A taxicab drew in under the lights below and surprisingly the driver got out quickly and opened the cab door. Courtesy of that kind New York is as significant as a knife between the ribs. The driver helped his passenger out—an old man. He carried an umbrella and a briefcase and his side-whiskers under the brim of his silk hat stood out like pom-poms on the rump of a white poodle. He paid the driver meticulously from a clasp purse and looked up at the doorway of 212. The driver took his arm and helped him across to the door. A moment later, the bell in the apartment behind Mat buzzed. He punched the buzzer and opened the hall door, leaning over the stair-rail.

"Mr. Davanan?" somebody called up from below.

"Yes"—from some instinct he started down the stairs. The old fellow stood below, looking up at him.

He was old, that quiet super age when all physical action is a definite result of meticulous thought. His step was firm, but slow. His green umbrella was tightly furled, his gray silk gloves buttoned carefully, his old-fashioned canvas brief-case buckled and tucked closely under his left arm.

The old man smiled up at Mat.

"Mr. Matthew Lloyd Davanan?"

"Yes, sir," Mat said.

"I'm Andrew Goldsboro," and he started slowly up the stairs. Mat stepped backwards up the two or three steps he had come down and opened the apartment door. He stood there while the old man came up.

Andrew Goldsboro put his brief-case on the table, his silk hat carefully on top of it, the umbrella beside them and began to peel off his gray silk gloves. Mat stood behind him waiting for his caped coat. He had the comfortably drooped face of a Basset hound. It hung from the line of his silver hair to his cravat, in long loose folds of pink flesh. His eye-sockets had loosened below his eyeballs into moist pink triangles, but the eyes themselves were still alert, young almost and intensely amused by the fact that they alone had stayed young enough to laugh at the spectacle of Old Andrew Goldsboro still walking abroad in the world and doing his chores.

With his coat off, he stood before Mat in gray-striped wor-steds and a snugly buttoned Prince Albert.

"Please sit down," Mat said.

"I trust you will overlook the informality of my call," the old man said, "but I find that at my age, my mind is clearer at night than in the daytime. I took the afternoon train up from Baltimore and I have just arrived."

Andrew Goldsboro cleared his throat, took a large linen handkerchief from his breast pocket, wiped his lips carefully and looked at Mat.

"I have come to inform you that you have inherited York Seat, sir. And this, sir, is the third time in my lifetime that I have said that to a Davanan. It gives one a sense of the inexorability of time. As a very young man, my father sent me to Mr. Edward Davanan to inform him. I was always Mr. Charles Davanan's lawyer. I told him when Mr. Edward died. And now, I tell you."

"I still don't understand it," Mat said.

"Mr. Charles Davanan's—your great-uncle's—will leaves it to you as the only surviving Davanan. I wrote to you on Charles Davanan's death, but received no reply."

"I didn't get the letter," Mat said. "It's a damned shame you had to make this trip, sir."

"Not at all. I like it," the old man smiled. "It gives one a sense of importance—traveling on trains."

Mat loved him.

Andrew Goldsboro said: "When I looked into it and found you had not answered the original letter, I had the police locate you for me to see if I had the right address."

Mat said, "And the right Davanan."

"I trust the police didn't annoy you."

"Not at all. This is an amusing story."

"Oh, quite usual—I assure you."

"I mean that I should come into York Seat."

"Good Lord, sir, why shouldn't you? Your family's had it since Baltimore's time. And the Davanans have always been family mad."

"Yes, but you don't know my branch of the family. Or do you?"

"You refer to your grandfather?"

"Naturally."

"He had a club-foot, you know. His mother and father were double first cousins. She was a Carrollton Carroll. That close a degree of blood relationship in marriage generally is unwise.

Your grandfather I knew well at one time. He wasn't as black as people liked to paint him. He was a gentleman, sir."

"Just exactly what did he do?"

"Principally, he mulcted his older brother, your great-uncle Charles. It started in a whist feud at the Maryland Club and it ended by your grandfather selling a vast amount of stock to Charles Davanan—in a gold mine in Nevada—a gold mine that Charles was still trying to locate, I expect, when he died."

"What about the boarding-house-keeper's daughter—my sainted grandmother?"

"She was a very beautiful girl." Andrew Goldsboro smiled. "Of course, keeping a boarding-house in Baltimore three generations ago was slightly more of a social impediment than it is to-day," his eyes twinkled, "but then, personally, while its social position is impeccable, I have never considered the British Royal Family to be what we call family, in Maryland. Your grandmother was a Pinckney." Andrew Goldsboro said: "But we get away from the subject in hand." He took out a great gold turnip of a watch. "I must get the eleven o'clock train back for I like to sleep in my own bed and I open the office at eight these days to get my mail attended to before the day starts. I have one or two papers for your signature—" He started to get up for his brief-case.

"Tell me, Mr. Goldsboro—do you know anything about a woman named Madeleine Bligh Vom Bloercke?" Mat asked him. "She wants to rent York Seat. She was referred to me here."

Old Andrew's eyes twinkled.

"Yes, yes,—I sent her. Charming soul."

"Who were the Blighs—were they connected with us? There is a Bligh River near York Seat. It's mentioned in *Eastern Shore Manor Houses.*"

"I never heard of the family, sir. The Bligh River was named for Bligh in Gloucestershire, England, I believe. Where your family came from."

"What do you know about a Lord Innes?"

"I've met him—and his secretary, a lovely girl. He wants to look over the old burial records."

"Yes. He thinks Napoleon is buried in the cemetery at York Seat."

Andrew Goldsboro chuckled. "For all I know, Napoleon may be there with all the rest. That cemetery holds a heterogeneous collection. Admiral Badenoch, two baker's dozens of Davanans—a half a dozen bodies from the ship *Mary and Anna* which went on Wreck Point in the seventeen hundreds and the Lord of Hosts knows who else."

"And there's an old yacht—I have a letter here somewhere from the Baltimore Scrap Iron Company—wanting to buy it."

"Don't you sell it!" Andrew Goldsboro said. "They'll only break it up and ship it to Japan for munitions. It deserves a better fate; that's Abe Laredo's *Paphos.*"

Old Andrew opened his brief-case and laid a book on the table top. "There is a book you must read. *The Gay Laredo,* by Anthony Dwight Bresson. I've marked certain passages. Abe Laredo was your great-great-uncle by marriage. Read between the lines and you'll never sell that yacht—you'll have it set in concrete as a monument to a magnificent pirate! Abe was a very gay boy. He built the *Paphos* in the late eighties. She must have been perfect hell at sea, high and narrow, but Abe went everywhere in her. His famous gold-plated bed was still in the owner's state-room the only time I was aboard. The *Paphos* went to Sonja, Charles Davanan's wife, when Abe died in 1893 in Villefranche. She and Charles crossed the Atlantic in her. That was in 1894, a foul winter that year. They carried Charles off on a stretcher in Baltimore and he lay six weeks in hospital getting over the trip. They sent the boat over to York Seat and never used it again. Don't you sell that boat!"

Mat laughed. "All right—if you say so, sir."

"And now," Old Andrew stood up and reached for his brief-case, "I have two releases here that I would like your signature on nowand I trust that the next time we meet, it will be at York Seat."

"I shall go down, naturally," Mat said, "as soon as I can."

"I wonder," the old man turned and looked at him solemnly, "if you can possibly know how satisfying that will be to me?" Andrew Goldsboro inclined his head. "To see a Davanan at York Seat—instead of the Daughters of the Confederacy. Charles Davanan might have willed it to them for a museum, you know," he sighed. "They talk so much, sir. Admirable ladies—but ladies with a Purpose—and I find that ladies who have attained the years of dignity, shall we say, and who in so doing have acquired a Purpose, and a taste for elderberry wine, can be most talkative. And having attained the years of dignity myself I find all talk depressing—except, of course, my own."

Mat laughed. Andrew Goldsboro got out his papers and spread them on the table for Mat's signature. Mat signed them and the old man put them back in his brief-case.

"And now, sir, I have a bare quarter hour more in which to complete my business with you." Andrew Goldsboro sat down again.

"Mr. Matthew," he folded his hands, "as one grows older in life, one learns to save excess motion—both physically and mentally. I have known your great-uncle Charles for the seventy-four years of his lifetime. As a boy, I used to spend weeks at York Seat visiting his older brother Edward. In those days, young Charles Davanan was what children call a sissy. He had a weak throat and chest. He never joined in our games, never rode, or sailed, or swam—and his father didn't even suggest a gun to him when he became old enough to handle one. He gave him a paint-box instead. Charles Davanan read Keats, Shelley, and Rossetti while Edward and I swilled our first flaming mouthfuls of Maryland Rye against the fall bitterness and crouched in the blinds off Wreck Point, blazing away at the best food Maryland produces, filling our bags to overflowing. At sixteen, Charles Davanan went negligently and delicately to Rome to study architecture. In his early twenties, he was the best-dressed fop at the Bachelors' Cotillions. At twenty-seven, in London, he married Sonja Laredo, whose dot was fifteen millions of dollars. Thereafter, the Charles Davanans became the scintillating focal point for that rather unsavory olla podrida that is called International Society to-day. They patroned the anemic arts and fed hungry nobility. Charles wrote delicately worded monographs on the pre-Rapha-elites and the general obligation of intelligent people to abhor all the crudities that were America. His accent, always precise, became so precious that I doubt if his own tenant farmers could have understood one word that he spoke. They lived in a villa at Frascati, in Sonja's London house in Cavendish Square, and at Abe Laredo's monstrous palace near L'Etoile. You won't believe it, but Abe Laredo used to light that house with eleven thousand candles, replaced daily, with new ones. In my lifetime, I haven't seen as much money as his bill for candles ran to during one Paris race season." Old Andrew smiled. "Nor have I seen a Paris race season."

"South African diamond money, wasn't it?"

"It started there, then it become oil, a large share of the Rothschild's banking interests—and Malayan rubber. Abe Laredo was the first of the genial financial pirates."

Mat nodded.

"The few times he returned to Baltimore in the forty years he lived abroad, I always saw Charles Davanan. He was a tall, slender, delicately turned man, precise to a detail. When he was still Sonja's husband, his personal suite consisted of his secretary, his barber-valet and his cook. He never ate anything that his own cook didn't prepare—in clubs, hotels, or private houses. It was almost impossible to get him to speak English. He preferred French. He was that complete miscegenation of leisure and over-bred ego—the dilettante. He spoke beautifully on every subject—but said nothing. Is it likely that such a man would come three thousand miles to the Eastern Shore of Maryland in October to shoot duck on Wreck Point—at seventy-four years of age—when he had never shot a duck in his life?"

Mat looked startled. "Is that what he did?"

"That's what they will have us believe he did."

"How did he die?"

"He didn't die—he was killed!"

There was no intent to shock, in old Andrew Goldsboro. He made the statement simply—as a statement of legal fact which it was necessary to make.

"What's been done about it?"

"The same things have been done about it that have been done many times before, I'm afraid," Andrew Goldsboro said. "The States Attorney for the County and the Sheriff and the local doctor they use for their Medical Examiner over there, have concurred in the opinion that he met his death accidentally, that he stumbled—and his gun went off. He was buried in the York Seat graveyard. The authorities accepted the local verdict. They didn't know Charles Davanan well. I do not accept it. When you can go down to York Seat, I propose that you and I investigate the matter personally, for the sake of the family."

"Why would any one want to kill him?"

"That has me," Andrew Goldsboro frowned slightly. "There was no money worth a murder. Sonja Laredo divorced him in 1906, two years before she died, and gave him an ample trust fund for his lifetime, but no power on earth could break that trust. It was made in London and has reverted to the Laredo interests. Charles Davanan's total assets outside of that trust were a few thousand a year from his brother Edward's will—and York Seat. He was too old a man to be embroiled with a woman. What other reasons for murder have we?"

"I don't know—"

"Well, we shall see—when you can come to Maryland. And now, good night to you, sir."

CHAPTER FIVE

A FTER the old man had gone, Mat opened the book. There were half a dozen markers in it—long strips of yellow paper. On the top of the first marked page was the word "yacht?" In pencil and below it, underlined in the text:

One of the first international pirates of finance in this modern era, there was scarcely a civilized country in the world where Laredo's funds were not invested at one time or another. An intellect of fabulous scope in conceiving and carrying out new enterprises, he never lost touch with the smallest detail of any of his businesses. He could walk into his offices in New York, Penang, Saigon, or Cape Town, ask for the books, spend an hour with them and know as much about the smallest items as his local manager knew. Sir Marcus Cohen, his personal attorney in later years, once said that he had no idea why Abe retained him, for he himself drew every contract and agreement he ever made with a clarity, brevity, and simplicity that beggared description and that needed no legal mumbo-jumbo added to it to make it perfect.

A sentimentalist to the core, Abe amply supported the remotest members of his family with trust funds, all of which agreements he drew himself with the principals invariably returnable on death to the Laredo interests, The Royal Cape Trading Company.

Opposite that notation, Old Andrew had written in pencil: "As was the principal of Charles Davanan's trust fund."

The text was marked further:

Laredo so prided himself on his credit, that he made it a point never to carry money in his pocket. Having started life as a colliery whelp in Dangollen without a penny, he gave this sop to his vanity throughout his lifetime. He was never known to pay cash for the smallest necessity and this idiosyncrasy being well known, he was seldom required to.

And besides that, Old Andrew had penciled: "So if it is the yacht, there can't be money on it, can there? And when did the Davanans ever have money they didn't spend at once?"

Old Andrew had combed through the book—looking for anything that might conceivably point to an objective for any one's illicit operations at York Seat.

Mat turned twenty pages to the next marker and the next underlining of the text:

Laredo knew what jewels cost men in work, suffering, and privation and he detested, as a business man, the thought of vast amounts of capital being crystallized in small, physical bulk. He never purchased a jewel or jewelry for himself or any of his gallant ladies. His own accessories he invariably had made in steel, his favorite metal, and when he was definitely out of his Kimberley interests and well on his way to giving Deterding and Rockefeller a run for the world's oil, he refused to receive ladies who wore jewels. He was more rabid on this subject than Thomas Alva Edison was on perfume.

And in Old Andrew's handwriting: "Nor can there be a hidden horde of jewels. Why murder, then?"

Mat turned to the next marker:

Abe Laredo left two daughters of record, and probably several other children not on any records. Sonja Laredo, who married a Mr. Charles Davanan of Baltimore, was born in Paris to his wife on June 13, 1870. Abe's second daughter was born to the Honorable Helen Forsythe in the Victoria Hospital near Nice on August 8, 1878, without benefit of anything nearer clergy than a magnificent trust fund for the Honorable Helen, and the most accomplished Harley Street gynecologists Abe's money could retain. In 1904 that daughter married Lord Astley-Thorndike, who was then approaching his seventy-fifth year. He sued her for divorce two years later by naming as corespondent Lord Challoner's heir. The divorce was granted for two very sound reasons at law. The first, that whereas Lord Astley-Thorndike had spent the thirteen months previous to the suit at his place at Crail in Scotland, his wife had spent them in the Villa Nid d'Aigle at Beaulieu. And the second, that he had been reliably informed that she had presented him with a daughter two weeks before he instituted suit.

It was the Honorable Helen's daughter, the sub-rosa mother of that sub-rosa granddaughter, that Abe is supposed to have offered a half-a-million pounds to for the return of diaries in her possession.

So much bilge, all of it, to Mat. He chucked the whole thing for the night.

He got Lord Innes' letter about luncheon the first thing the next morning and called Anne Langdon.

Her voice, when he got her, was contained, impersonal. She was not being the efficient secretary with him. She was herself— but a cool, detached self. She's thought that kiss over and decided against it—she's embarrassed by it.

"You're fairly stiff," he laughed. "Have you forgotten that you and I used to make mud pies together? What's the matter—can't you talk? Is some one there?"

"No."

"Anything more on last night?"

"No," she said, "except the police have taken prints from the foot of the bed. You'll be here for luncheon?" Cold—like that.

"Yes."

He had a week more of his vacation coming to him. He put the bee on B. K. to let him have that week now—and he must have caught B. K. right, for he got it. Then he got Tommy Powell on the telephone at one of Tommy's refilling stations and got Tommy's car for a week—and took a cab to the St. Daviston for luncheon.

Lord Innes was up and about. He had one of the finest heads Mat had even seen. So unbelievably fine that it was startling on his body for that was a slight body, infinitely delicate. Almost an apologetic body, if you will, draped loosely in tweeds, ages old. Not sickly, for there was strength in the lines of it, but the strength of a violin string perhaps or of a scalpel—a fine machine that could be smashed with a blow, as completely as a watch can be smashed or a precision instrument in a laboratory. All the awkwardness of peasantry—the heaviness, the crudeness had been bred out of Lord Innes leaving nothing but quintessential grace. But an intensely masculine grace, that was no more out of place in the St. Daviston than it would have been two centuries ago at Versailles. Like the Macdonald—where Lord Innes sat was the head of the table, and his head above it was a piece of exquisite sculpture, complete, finished in every line—beautifully burined.

Approaching sixty, Lord Innes had his world fairly well licked, Mat felt, by the simple process of living beyond it in the fortress of his own mind. The startling beauty of his head protected him from intrusion. Strangers saw its old aristocracy, stepped aside, bowed slightly and went on.

But amazingly, his voice denied it all. It was not a particularly English voice—international rather, with no exaggeration of accent—and it was low in pitch and somewhat halting, as if he expected contradiction, needed it almost, to stimulate him to go on speaking.

"It was kind of you, Mr. Davanan, to come here to luncheon"—almost a question.

They had luncheon in his suite, twenty-two stories above New York. In Lord Innes' presence Anne Langdon was a different person entirely—the paid secretary. She did that easily with complete self-control.

She was like that—an entity to herself, and it was an amazing thing suddenly to Mat that he had held her in his arms and kissed her. An impossible thing that had never happened to them—for they were almost strangers now with no part in each other's lives.

The realization of that hit him so hard for a moment that he was afraid it showed in his face, for his whole body was empty with it suddenly. For a moment the nostalgia he had felt in the taxi yesterday came back to him like a physical blow.

Through it, he had the sudden feeling that their intruder of the evening before was not to be spoken of. Police orders perhaps—perhaps their own shock at the incident. He comes in with a gun and says "No—not this time. I'm warning you." And he leaves. From then on—the police. It's a closed incident.

After the second try Mat gave it up and listened to Lord Innes.

"... and then, Sir, there was the attempt by submarine which is most interesting. The submarine was to be towed in close to shore at high tide and dropped, submerged. At low tide, Napoleon was to go aboard it and close himself into it—and it was to be picked up at high tide again by its marking buoy and Napoleon taken aboard the ship. The submarine was probably no more than a large, water-tight barrel with chambers that could be flooded."

Mat said: "And you think he got away from St. Helena in that submarine, and came to America?"

"No," Lord Innes shook his head, "that attempt was undoubtedly a failure. What I think happened was that one of his impersonators, an actor named Chaqueville, made his way to St. Helena, substituted himself for the exiled Emperor and allowed Napoleon to escape as a sailor in the brig *Porteus*."

"But why York Seat, Sir—where does my family enter into the scheme of things? You mentioned a Robert Davanan in your letter to me—"

"Yes," Lord Innes nodded. "Robert Davanan was a shipping man. He had a wheat ship impounded at St. Nazaire in 1803. He fought the impounding for three years in the Paris courts personally through pique. But in those three years there was no one of importance in Paris that he didn't meet. He became rabidly Napoleonic and invested a great deal of money in France. He made a great fortune which he lost, of course, after Waterloo— but his friendship for Napoleon and Marshal Bernadotte always remained intact. I believe the brig *Porteus* made its way to Baltimore and that there, Robert Davanan met his friend Napoleon Bonaparte and took him to York Seat where he lived to the end of his days as 'Mr. Bertrand'—and where he is buried."

"And it was the letters of that Robert Davanan to Marshal Bernadotte that put you on this trail?"

Lord Innes nodded.

"I would like to see those letters."

"I would like you to."

"Have you them here?"

"Unfortunately, no."

"It's the damndest story I ever heard," Mat said.

"Oh, no," Lord Innes laughed. "The damndest story about bones that any one has ever heard is the story of the bones of Columbus. They were buried in Spain and consequently when they were found in the apse of the Cathedral of Santo Domingo about forty years ago and the Spanish Consul General claimed them in the name of Spain—he was recalled in disgrace for daring to insinuate that the bones were not already in Spain. It ruined the man's diplomatic career."

"Suppose you find the bones—how can you identify them?"

"I have pieced together from the records a complete medical history of Napoleon—his wounds and malformations and fractures." Lord Innes smiled. "I am doing this purely for my personal amusement—and to confound the French, whom I loathe."

Mat said, "Let's get right after it, shall we? I have borrowed a car from a friend of mine. If you're well enough, we can start tomorrow. I can drive—but I haven't a license." He turned to Anne. "Have you a license?"

"Yes—"

"Well, that's that then," Mat said. "How soon do you think you'll be able to travel, Lord Innes?"

"But I'm afraid my license has expired," Anne said. "I'm sure it has. I wasn't here—to renew it." Mat looked at her sharply. Her voice was strained again as it had been on the telephone.

Lord Innes said, "I shall be able to go tomorrow. Can you drive us, Miss Langdon?"

"I—I can drive all right. But I'm not sure about my license—and the penalties are very strict in America—"

"How long ago did you take the license out?" Mat asked her.

"About—two years ago," she said.

"In New York?"

"Yes, in New York," she nodded.

"They're good for three years without renewal."

"But I'm not sure I can find it," Anne said helplessly.

"Well, you can sit in front with me," Mat grinned, "and when I hit other cars, you can talk the policeman out of it."

Lord Innes had the happy faculty of pursuing his own thoughts relentlessly with no regard for the side alleys that other people's conversation explored, and Mat suddenly realized that he did it because he was slightly deaf.

Mat watched him closely and when he looked out of the window a moment, he said to the girl in a low voice, "Why don't you want to go to Maryland?"

The color rose to her cheeks, but she didn't answer him.

"You don't like me to-day at all, do you?" he said.

"Do be quiet."

"What have I done?"

Lord Innes' delicate body was tiring and the curiosity was gone from him with his fatigue. He sipped his luncheon coffee absently. Presently he said:

"To-morrow then, Mr. Davanan—at what time?"

"Early—I suggest—say ten sharp? That will get us down to the Eastern Shore in time for dinner."

"I shall be ready. You are very kind to allow me the freedom of the York Seat library."

"I hope we find one. After all," Mat grimaced, "rats can eat a lot of books in forty years."

Lord Innes didn't hear the quip. "Ah, yes—one other thing. I suggest that I become merely Mr. Montgomery down there, Mr. Davanan. Rural communities are, I find, actively impressed by any other label the fates put on a man."

"As you say, Sir." They shook hands and Lord Innes looked at Anne.

"Miss Langdon will see you out."

As Mat walked with the girl into the tiny hall, he said: "I want to talk to you alone."

"No," she shook her head.

"Look here. You've got something on your mind. What is it?"

"Not a thing."

"Why don't you want to go to Maryland?"

"I do want to—I want to get out of New York as soon as I can."

"Why?"

"I'm frightened."

"Of what?"

"Of everything—since last night. Please put on your coat and go. After all, I'm an employee here. I can't chat endlessly with you."

"Will you see me to-night?"

"I can't—I have to work here."

"So you won't talk?" He shrugged into his coat. She put a hand on his arm suddenly and looked up at him.

"What?"

"I don't know," she said helplessly.

"When you do—will you tell me?" he smiled.

Her face was solemn. "If I can."

CHAPTER SIX

IT was getting on toward late afternoon as Mat walked over slowly to 58th Street and east to his apartment. The fall evening was coming down on New York, in blue mist. It was that hour of the day when all the sharp corners are gone from the buildings and people run out from their day's slavery and scuttle onto busses and into subways to go back to the holes they live in. Fantasy in the air, transcending reality in soft colors and neon lights and the muffled snort of traffic—and for a few minutes Mat had the illusion of ghosts in the crowds at Fifth Avenue and 59th—the swaggering ghosts of all yesterdays—men in stocks with bottle-green tailcoats, ladies in mitts and bonnets. This town had the news of Waterloo and read it avidly as it was reading the latest murder mystery now. Maybe his own ancestor Robert Davanan had walked the streets of it. Captain the Honorable Eric Molleston might quite possibly have lain off there in the North River on the decks of the *Duchess of Gordon* as a midshipsmite in 1777.

Tommy Powell, clapping him on the shoulder, broke the illusion.

"And how is the wholesome Anne Langdon to-day," Tommy boomed at him. "A lovely, pristine job of work, my boy, with nice hair and a cool eye and an unstudied sense of female efficiency you can believe in—but I'll turn her up. Never fear, I'll place her. I'll put her in her slot."

"She's Dorothy Arnold," Mat snorted at him.

"She's somebody, Old Boy. Never fear, Old Powellsywowellsey never goes wrong on a face."

"You've gone wrong this time. Nobody could be more in the clear. Look her up if you want to. She's got a New York driver's license now to add to the other exhibits she offered."

They walked over to 212 together and went up to the apartment and let themselves in.

Mat dusted an opera hat, a suitcase, one shoe, and a typewriter off his couch, and lay down full length. All the clothes Tommy owned lay on the floor in front of his closet. Somebody had built a magpie's nest under the desk—pipes, papers, an empty bottle, a Princeton stein, a glove—and the ink spilled comfortingly over all of it.

"I suppose we ought to speak to O'Bannion about this mess," Mat said. "I've been out of here since nine this morning—and here it is almost five and she hasn't cleaned up yet. What is it exactly that we pay her for, do you remember—her charm?"

"I was just thinking," Tommy said. "I was undoubtedly stiff last night, but I don't remember throwing all my clothes on the floor. And what about the desk?"

"You weren't here last night," Mat told him. "You don't quite understand the function of this apartment, in its relationship to your private life. This is where you shave and keep your clean shirts."

Tommy stood in the middle of the room. "I believe you're right," he said. "I went to the zoo last night with an old friend from Cincinnati—but I was here this morning. I wrote a check at that desk before I went out again—and the pigeonholes were full. They're slicked clean now—everything's on the floor including the ink!"

"What the hell do you mean?" Mat raised himself on both elbows.

"I mean we've been gone through," Tommy said. "Had. Taken."

There was a knock at the door. Tommy opened it. Mrs. O'Bannion their cleaning woman.

47

"Can I do the place now, Mr. Powell?"

"If you can find it under this mess. Come in, Mrs. O'Bannion. Have you been in the house all day?"

"I was here late this morning—but your friend told me to come back to clean."

"What friend?"

"The tall man who slept here last night. Mr. Davanan's friend," he said.

"Nobody slept here but me," Mat told her.

"Well, he was here this morning after you left," Mrs. O'Bannion said. "He told me to come back later. Said he'd slept here—you'd put him up for the night."

"What'd I tell you, Mat! Somebody's been through this pot-house from top to bottom."

"Anything missing?" Mrs. O'Bannion said.

Mat sat up suddenly. "Mrs. O'Bannion, what'd this man look like?"

"Like a tall man looks, I guess."

"I see," Mat nodded, "wearing an American Legion hat, ballet slippers, a track suit and carrying the tops of two Ford cars he'd just torn off to send in to the Contest Editor."

"I didn't notice none of that."

"What did you notice?"

"He was just going out."

"How do you know?"

"He had his hat on."

"Good! What else."

"His coat, too."

"What have you got, Mat?"

"Even money—but I don't know why—that the guy who did this job was the same guy who went through Lord Innes' at the St. Daviston last night."

"You're crazy."

"I've never said I wasn't, have I?"

"No. You've been very good about that." Tommy picked up the telephone book. "We're Fourth Detective District here, aren't we?" He thumbed through, got the number, and grabbed the phone.

They got a dick named Osser about seven o'clock.

"You're foolish," Osser said. "What would a guy who works a flash dump like the St. Daviston be working a place like this for, too?"

"You tell me," Mat said. "I'm in the earthworm business myself. The point is, he didn't work either place. Nothing's gone."

Tommy said, "My old father here gets one hunch a year, but when he does—he gets them. If you wanta be smart—check with whoever is on the St. Daviston job."

"No use," Osser said, "foolish. No connection."

"All right—if you don't ever get to be Commissioner, don't say we didn't give you a chance."

Mat said, "Now look, you don't have to do this if you don't want to, but it's easy to do and easy to forget about, if it doesn't jell. A guy named Lord Innes at the St. Daviston was gone through last night and the detective on the job over there has turned up prints on the bed. You give that desk there a going over and if you find any prints on it but Powell's or mine—compare them with the St. Daviston prints. If they are the same as the St. Daviston prints—you've got a mystery at least and you may win second place in the Canoe-Tilt. Who can tell?"

"Who can?" Osser said. "Who ever can?"

"That's what I always say," Tommy said. "What do you always say?"

Osser said, "Nuts usually."

"A very sound practice," Mat nodded. "And now, Mr. Osser— if you would like my fingerprints, they are yours for the asking but you must promise me that I won't be indicted for the First National Bank job."

"You guys would be on some paper if memory serves me," Osser said.

"Impertinent I calls it," Tommy said.

CHAPTER SEVEN

THEY got an eleven o'clock start the next morning, bag and baggage with Lord Innes in a tweed Connaught, tucked in his tartan steamer rugs in back, with Mat driving and Anne sitting in front with him. Through the Holland Tunnel and over the Pulaski Skyway and into the south Jersey groove, heading for Pennsville Ferry. They made the three o'clock ferry to New Castle, Delaware, and had a bite of luncheon at the Black Cat. At Smyrna, they turned west for the Maryland line.

As soon as they were well out of traffic Mat said:

"We got it yesterday."

"Got what?"

"An inquisitive caller," he said, "at the apartment. Only he dropped in when we weren't in. Nobody saw him but O'Bannion of the Dust Pans."

Anne looked at him quickly. "You mean somebody broke into your apartment?"

"Just that," Mat nodded. The girl closed her hands tightly in her lap.

"—and apparently," Mat went on, "he did the same thing there that he did with you people at the St. Daviston. Took just exactly nothing."

"Why do you speak about it," Anne asked him, "as if it were the same man?"

"Because," Mat told the girl, "I have an insane hunch that it was the same man and I told our detective to check on the theory."

"You shouldn't have done that," she said sharply.

"Why not?"

"I don't know," her eyes were troubled. "But you shouldn't have. The man who forced his way in on us was an extremely dangerous man. I can still feel the chill in his words."

"All the more reason why the police should turn him up."

"No," she said firmly, "the police can't do anything."

"Why not?"

"I don't know." And after that she wouldn't talk. That is, she would talk about anything but what Mat wanted to talk about, so he stopped trying. No give. Where'd you go to school? All over. Always live in New York? Goodness, no. Father never stayed in one place more than four months. New Orleans, San Francisco, Arizona, Acapulco.

"All right," Mat said. "The woman of mystery."

"There is no mystery about it at all!" she said sharply.

"All right, all right—don't get angry."

"I'm not angry."

Mat said, "You've simply decided that you're not having any—that's it, isn't it?"

"What do you mean?"

He said, "Let's be frank. On thinking it all over, you've decided you made a mistake kissing me in the taxi two days ago. You want to forget it," he spread his hands. "All right, we shall forget it. Be a cad—and see if I care. That's a very pretty red cow over there in the field, isn't it—a very pretty red cow—isn't it?"

The Eastern Shore of Maryland is flat country and, if you like the music in the word, desolate. It lies west and south of Delaware between the Atlantic and the Chesapeake Bay, a seven hours' drive from New York. In the summer it bakes a crisp brown and in the winter, salt mists shroud it and the dampness rots the red earth of the back roads into viscous glue. But in the spring and in the fall there is no more delightful country in America. It is Scottish moors then, after the grouse have departed—or the ancient coast of Kent—with the same yeoman ghosts at twilight. It is Flemish France without the Spanish farms of Alba. But to love it there must be mists in your own soul—a memory of old fogs in your nostrils—the instinct to love good dogs and to see stark beauty in the swift flight of birds in the rain.

In late October, when Mat Davanan saw it first, night comes down briskly like a lank farm woman striding through the dusk and the faces one sees in its blue darkness become old faces. Faces pondering the tragedy of Braddock's men, lying with flies on their dead lips in the great forests of Western Virginia, their bodies swelling to burst their scarlet coats—because the General wouldn't listen to Will Washington's boy. Faces grinning at the news of the surrender, brought by Tench Tilghman from Yorktown. Faces horrified at the Shiloh defeat, jubilant over Château-Thierry.

There are scabrous, whitewashed Negro towns, popping up suddenly through the leafless trees around the next bend of the road. Deserted meeting-camps. Children plodding homeward alone from school, to isolated farms. Old brick villages called Church Hill and Princess Anne, St. Michaels, and Royal Oak, their age disturbed by gasoline pumps and Coca-Cola signs and ten-cent stores. There is a hunter in a red cap, climbing a fence, with his brown retriever far ahead of him. There is a banner in the next town, "Turkey Shoot," an old Negro on the empty road, touching his battered hat as the car flashes by—a softening drawl in white men's voices—wood smoke in the twilit air—an oyster boat chugging in to the cannery wharf—and far away through the trees, the mild Georgian slope of ancient gables, the soft tone of hand-baked brick and the shabby oaks of a long-forgotten carriage oval.

Intangibly, it got Mat. Some people are like that. Virginia will do it. Connemara. Perhaps it's the nebulous ghost of all your old people when you are in their country. The spiritual feeling that it has all been done before—that as you have gone to school, so have other little boys before you, in buckskin knee-breeches and tricorne and pewter-buckled shoes. Little boys who have grown up to become Justices of the Peace under a long dead Duke of York—who have had other drip-nosed little boys who grew up to be howling, sword-waving Majors of the Maryland Line at Brooklyn and Brandywine and Cowpens, who had other little boys who just grew fat over their port and had still other little boys who ran away from the tedium of Cæsar's Gallic Wars at St. John's College at Annapolis to choke on a minnie ball at Manassas and die quite young and alone in a brand-new gray jacket that had looked so nice to the pink-cheeked girls a few weeks before—girls who had miraculously been grandmothers in your own time and died with all their memories, before you yourself were quite grown up. Mat reversed it all, with sundown. All those old Davanans became his children and he was excessively fond of them.

It was after five when they arrived at the Chincoteague Hotel in the County Seat—a low frame building with broad verandas that faced Court House Square and the Confederate Memorial opposite. There were two stairways in the old hotel, one for ladies in hoop skirts and the other for gentlemen. The clerk pointed that out to them, standing with his back to a bronze plaque on the wall, "Rotary International. Every Thursday at 12." He was very proud of that staircase. It meant something to him culturally—he didn't know quite what—and he wanted to show them the old hotel register, when they liked his staircase, but Mr. Montgomery was tired and wanted his room. Mr. Montgomery looked tired. His delicate body drooped slightly at the shoulders and his face was drawn from the long ride down. Nervous energy there, Mat felt—that would drive the old man furiously to any goal he set out to achieve—but in doing it, it drained the strength from his slight body to a point of complete exhaustion. His eyes apologized for it.

Up in his own room, Mat picked up the telephone and asked for Information. "I want the telephone of Mr. Andrew Goldsboro,

24 Ferris Street, Baltimore. He's a lawyer. Yes—I'll hold on." He sat on the bed, tapping the instrument with his fingernails, waiting, and he knew suddenly exactly what Andrew Goldsboro's Law Office was like. It would have a double clerk's desk at one side, with high stools for the clerks. At the other side would be Andrew Goldsboro's old-fashioned desk, with dozens of dusty legal volumes behind, bound in crumbling tan cowhide. There would be a cuspidor, no carpet, a heroic lithograph of Calhoun and old Andrew Goldsboro would always answer his own telephone himself as a matter of courtesy.

The operator said: "The number is Calvert 4840."

"Ring it, will you?"

He heard her get through to Baltimore, heard the Baltimore operator start to say something, and then he was clicked off at his end. In a moment, the operator said: "I'm sorry, Sir—but there is no answer."

"Have you a residence number for the same name?"

"Not in Baltimore, sir."

"Well—that's that. Thanks," and he hung up. He called the operator again and had her put him on to Western Union and he sent this to old Andrew:

AM AT THE CHINCOTEAGUE HOTEL STOP ADVISE WHEN
YOU CAN MEET ME HERE

MATTHEW DANAVAN

Mat's mind was full of a slow excitement that made him restless. He reached for the road map they'd used coming down and spread it out on the bed. He located the Little Creek Road and measured off the distance from town. About thirteen miles. If there's a moon, I'll go out to York Seat to-night! He lit a cigarette and walked up and down the room for a moment, still restless. The air of the old town perhaps that his people had breathed for over two centuries. Everybody has ancestors, but when you know who they are, where they lived, they become entirely personal ancestors. You're not Smith or Jones any more—your name is a trademark that's been lived by before and you have a temporary right to it only. Your eyes are on yourself as a new arrival, wondering how you'll turn out.

He got up and changed his shirt, washed up for dinner, and went downstairs. There were a couple of salesmen in the lobby and the cheerful clerk.

"I was just looking at your name again," the clerk said. "It's kind of familiar around these parts."

Mat was on the point of saying: "It ought to be—" but the clerk got him first. "You aren't related to Al Davanan over in Denton, are you? I used to know Al well before he opened his butcher shop. He's doing fine, they tell me, and there was a cousin of his named Joe Davanan—a house-painter, worked for Raskob up at Centerville for a while—and for Chrysler. You know, the automobile man? They're the big families down here on the 'Shore.' Raskob and Chrysler. Joe Davanan got his hand cut off—thrashing. Married a fine girl from Easton though—she worked in Carson Riley's dog wagon. Swell girl."

Mat said: "There are some other Davanans who used to live near here, aren't there—at a place called York Seat? One of them used to be Governor of Maryland and another was Chief Justice of the Supreme Court in Madison's time." And as he said it, his mind flashed, "You damned snob" at him.

"Don't know about that," the clerk said. "York Seat is the name of an old place out near Wreck Point. A fellow name of Miers Buckmaster is the farmer. Lives on Big Creek Road. But nobody lives in the old house. It's going to be a museum some day, they say. Talbot Pyle can tell you about it. He's the State's Attorney here. His office is just across Court House Square." The clerk came out from behind the desk, walked to the door and opened it. "No lights in his windows," he said. "Guess he's closed up for the night," and he came back to the desk again. "Yeah.

York Seat," he said. "Lot of stories about that place. There was an old smugglers' run there or something that caved in. They got fences around it but it's kind of dangerous because nobody knows exactly where that passage was—or where the next cave-in'll be."

"I read about it," Mat said, "in the book. They call it the Captain's Run."

"Say, wait a minute," the clerk snapped his fingers. "Seems to me the fellow's name was Davanan who got killed out there ten days ago when I was in Wilmington. His gun went off while he was after duck. Seems to me the paper said he came over from Italy—but it don't sound like an Eyetalian name, does it? Mebbe it was Davanani."

"Maybe it was," Mat said.

"What line are you in?"

"Me?" Mat said. "I collect fish."

"Live ones?"

"No—dead ones. I stuff them and sell them to clubs."

CHAPTER EIGHT

A NNE LANGDON was coming down one of the parallel stairways. Mat raised a hand to her.

"Hello—how's the old boy?"

"Tired. He's gone to bed. I'm to send his dinner up to him."

"That means you're through for the night—" They went in to the dining-room and had their own dinner. "So how would you like to drive out to York Seat by moonlight?"

She looked at him.

"Just," he said firmly, "to see the place."

"Why not? I don't feel too tired—if you don't."

The evening air was brisk, after dinner. Sharp October air—like chilled Rhine wine. Somewhere deep in the little town, a melancholy church bell was ringing. There were footsteps in the blue darkness of the streets—dutiful ladies clacking off to Wednesday night prayer-meeting—calling to each other through the darkness. "Good evening, Mrs. Traymer. How is Mr. Traymer's arm?" The sound of a distant car snorted at the town in modern derision and the radio in Applethorp's drug-store on the corner was slightly blasphemous. There was a policeman at the garage—the night policeman. A callow youth in uniform trousers much too short for him, but with an important manner to strangers because the town's people gave him absolutely no importance.

"York Seat?" he said heavily. "Let me see now. You take State Route 112 out of town—that's the end of Queen Anne Street—two squares over and you turn left at the Bridge into Wreck Point

Road. Follow that about ten miles down to Thorpe's Corners and the Little Creek Road is a mile or two beyond it—to the right. York Seat's at the end of the Little Creek Road."

"What about a farmer named Buckmaster? Miers Buckmaster?"

"Oh, I know him," the youth said. "He don't live on Little Creek Road. He lives on Big Creek Road."

"Where's that?"

"Well, after you pass Little Creek Road—you go a mile farther down the Point and Big Creek Road makes off to the left. Miers' house is about half a mile in."

Anne started the car with Mat beside her with the map in his lap.

"You don't need that," she said.

"No?"

She shook her head. "I never get lost. Don't know why—but I never do. It's a gift. Father had it and I've got it." She turned out of Queen Anne Street into Route 112 and a few minutes later they roared across the Bligh River Bridge and took the left turn. Mat watched her. She drove relaxed as a man drives, a wisp of her hair under the scarf she had wound about her head trailing behind her.

He said, "You feel better to-night, don't you?"

She turned to him and smiled. "I love this place—the sleepy old town and the countryside. It makes you feel that no matter what happens to you in life, it's all happened to so many people before you that it can't matter much."

"Has much happened to you?"

"To me," she shook her head. "Not much really. I've had a fairly good life—so far."

The glow of the moon was hoar-frost in the tops of the bare trees that lined the road ahead of them. It bathed Anne's face, her smile; and it was so bright before they reached Thorpe's Corners that she could have snapped off her headlights.

"A crazy man—my father!" she laughed. "That was Thorpe's Corners we just passed through."

"Well, take it easy now," he said. "We've got a right-hand turn to look for. What do you mean, your father was a crazy man?"

"Just that," Anne threw her head back, smiling. "He lived naturally, that's all you have to do—to be crazy—or happy. He loved life enough to approach it simply. Most people hate it, you know, so they embellish it with all sorts of complications to make it palatable."

"Such as what?"

"The pretense of respectable friends—social codes—tailors, dressmakers, hair-dos, fine cars, smart luggage, lies, conceits, operations, correct addresses. Look here—we've gone two and a half miles beyond Thorpe's Corners and there's been no right turn that I've seen."

"Hold it—there's a break in the trees ahead to the left— that must be the Big Creek Road. Let's turn in there and see Miers Buckmaster." She ran down to the break and turned and after a few minutes there was a yellow pin point of light ahead. The road curved around to a clearing and there was a house presently and barns. Anne stopped the car and shut off the motor. A hound-dog started to bark and the night noises closed in on them, katydids and the heat crackle of their motor and there was the nitrous warmth in their nostrils of new manure. A door in the house opened into a sharp oblong of yellow light.

"Mr. Buckmaster?"

"Reckon so," a man's voice said. They could see him outlined against the light—a heavy, bent-shouldered man with great dangling hands. He came toward them.

"Good evening, I'm Matthew Davanan."

"What do you want?" Buckmaster was standing beside the car now, his face washed in the moon. A face painfully red with soap, shaved cleanly, with the dark hair combed down slick above it. He smelled wetly wormwoodish with dry perspiration and chewing tobacco.

"Well," Mat smiled, "I'm the man who owns York Seat."

"So?" Buckmaster said. His voice was soft but there was a finality to everything he said as if the conversation had stopped with each word and he was glad of it.

"Yes. I just got in from New York—I'm at the Chincoteague Hotel. It's early yet—so I thought I'd run out and have a look by moonlight. Are there any keys to the house?"

"I've got the keys," Buckmaster said. "Had 'em for twenty years. But I don't know you."

Mat said, "Well—a—"

"An' if I did," Buckmaster said, "I wouldn't take you up to York after nightfall."

Mat took out his pocket-book and handed Buckmaster his Amalgamated Press card.

Buckmaster held it up close to his eyes and looked at it in the light of the moon and handed it back.

"Well?" Mat said. "Will you give me the keys?"

"Nope," Buckmaster looked at him blandly. "No authority."

"What authority do you need?"

"Talbot Pyle."

"Can you telephone Pyle?"

"No telephone nearer than Thorpe's Corners."

"We'll run you up."

"Nope—too late."

"Look," Mat said patiently, "you farm the home farm here—and I'm the new owner. You'd like us to get along, wouldn't you?"

"A man ain't no use to another man if he ain't trustworthy," Buckmaster said. "You may be the new owner. You may not. Daylight'll tell. I wouldn't do anything to-night anyway—one way or the other. Not after dark."

"What do you mean? York Seat supposed to be haunted?"

"All the niggers'll tell you so."

"Nonsense."

Buckmaster said: "Mister—it won't do to fool around with nigger belief."

"What do they believe about it?"

"It's a hand-paralysin' ha'nt. Used to be a nigger-killin' overseer at York years ago. Whupped 'em to death. If you drive through the old gates after dark, you get hit across the whip hand and you can't ever move it again."

"Do you believe it?"

"Nope. And I don't have to because I don't ever go to York Seat after dark."

"I see. Well—I guess that's all for to-night then. I suppose if I bring you a note from Talbot Pyle to-morrow you'll be satisfied?"

"Yes," Buckmaster said.

"No hard feelings," Mat grinned.

"Course not," Buckmaster walked back to his house, went in and closed the door.

"The return," Anne said, "of the native. What do we do now?"

"We go to York Seat anyway."

"Right you are." She turned the car and ran back to the Wreck Point Road.

They're rather literal minded down here," she laughed. "Where does this road go? 'Wal I ben a settin' here twenty year and I ain't seen it move yet.' "

Mat laughed. "Listen—don't look a gift-house in the portico."

"I won't," she said, "but we didn't ask Miers about the Little Creek Road—"

"Well, it's got to be between here and Thorpe's Corners. The cop said so. Let's drive back slowly along Wreck Point Road and look for it."

"All right. Are you insured? Suppose we get our hands paralyzed?"

"Do you know," Mat said, "I have a distinctly uncanny feeling—that we won't."

She drove out of Big Creek and turned right on the Wreck Point Road and about half a mile back they saw a side road that they had missed coming from the opposite direction. Grass was grown across it and the new tree growth came out so close to the Wreck Point Road that it was just a lighter patch in the dark growth that lined the main road—a dark hole, leading into the darkness of the woods. Anne half turned in and stopped the car.

"Well?"

"This must be it," Mat said.

She shook her head. "It doesn't look too inviting. Soft, I'll bet, with that weed growth—and I get a feeling of rusty chains strung across it, don't you?"

"Take it slowly."

She started the car again and they joggled in, the weeds whipping the fenders like handfuls of thrown pebbles, the lights a yellow wash under the thick growth of trees.

"Look here," Anne said, "I don't like this road much. If we get mired down, who's going to push us out?"

"The answer is—don't get mired."

The car was bouncing under the interlaced arch of the branches above, groaning in second. The trees lined the hidden road ditches on either side at evenly spaced intervals. Beyond, on both sides, the fields lay silver in the full white light of the moon. After a quarter of a mile of it, Anne said:

"Those trees were planted this way. I wouldn't be surprised if this was an old carriage drive. Wait—" She stopped the car suddenly and pointed. On either side of the road, just ahead of them, there were high, vine covered gate-posts. Mat fumbled in the pocket of the instrument board and pulled out a flashlight. He snapped the beam on the posts—on the old weathered griffons on top of them—on the thickly clustered English ivy.

"I expect you're right," he said. "Let's go."

"We've got to," the girl shrugged, "we can't turn around—and we can't back out."

Anne started the car again. The road turned slightly and suddenly the car lights raked across closed bronze gates to the left. Beautiful gates they were, sweeping upward in gothic points—as foreign to the countryside as organ music. The tracery of them in the car lights had the exquisite delicacy of dry-point. Charles Davanan's contribution to York—the gates of the Borghese Palace he had brought from Rome forty years ago. Anne stopped the car.

"What now?"

"Well—I guess we'd better go on down the road until we find a place to turn—and come back."

Again Anne started the car and joggled on down under the trees. Presently, above the hot smell of the motor, they caught the damp breath of tide water. The trees overhead thinned out and through them in a moment, they saw the spreading gray metal of the moon on Bligh River. The road was considerably wider now but the ditches were uncertain depressions, thickly overgrown.

Suddenly, through the straggling trees, Mat saw the long gray bulk of a building. It was built well up the foreshore and extended out over the water about sixty feet. Two hundred feet long, perhaps, and sixty high—a long bulk of a building, brooding in its heavy silence, like a darkened armory. They got out of the car and walked toward it, their feet crunching loudly in the shale.

"It's a boat-house," Anne whispered.

"You know what's in it, don't you?"

"Rats, probably."

"Abe Laredo's yacht," Mat said. "The *Paphos*."

The boat-house was heavy and frowning, and as they came closer to it they saw that it was made of stone, on a heavy stone base—a hundred thousand dollars' worth of boat-house, easily. They climbed up on the base that ran around it and walked out along it toward the water end. When they came to the end, the stone base jutted beyond on either side, but between the two juts, there was a water slot in under the house, closed to its full height by great beamed doors. Mat leaned out, holding the girl's arm, and put his hand on them. They were heavy and studded and as sound still as the stone itself. The echo of his fist thumping them sprang across the water like a hollow cough, almost human.

They walked back and around to the other side. There was another door in back as sturdy as the water doors and as firmly bolted to its frame, as solid to Mat's fist when he thumped it.

"One boat-house, locked," Anne laughed, "supposed to be complete with boat. Check that off." And they walked back to the car. Anne turned the car around on the foreshore and headed it back the way they had come. She stalled in turning, and in the momentary silence, they heard a two-cycled marine motor chugging across the water. They could see the black shadow of a boat coming up the river from the bay. Mat touched the girl's arm to keep her from starting the car again, and they sat there for a few moments watching the boat head in the Bligh River. It was low in the water with a small cubby forward—an oysterman. It came up the river, slowly, a faint breath of air carrying its oily exhaust across to them, and abruptly the motor stopped chugging. With way on it, the boat moved ahead slowly until it was about two hundred feet off the front of the boat-house, then they saw the tall silhouette of a man standing up in her, and heard the splash of his kedge anchor going over the side. And that was all. The man must have sat down or crawled into the cubby, for his silhouette disappeared. The boat carried no lights, so there were no lights to go out on her now that she was on the hook. And apparently whoever was aboard her didn't believe in wasting oil on an anchor light.

"Well?" the girl said.

"Wait a minute," Mat opened the car door and got out. He stood there for a moment looking at the anchored boat, listening to the silence of the river, then he walked down to the water's edge, cupped his hands and shouted: "Aboard the oysterman!"

His voice echoed across the river and silence came down again heavily. There was a sound presently of wood on wood aboard the boat and again they saw the figure of the man standing up in it, silhouetted.

"Hello!" Mat called.

The man didn't answer him. It was the damndest thing. He just stood there in the boat, looking at him but not saying a word—and then, almost immediately, the boat's engine coughed into life again, the man hauled in his anchor and the boat headed out and up the river.

Anne said: "What were you going to say to him if he had answered you?"

"I'm damned if I know," Mat climbed in beside her again. "I expect that I've got a sudden sense of owning property. That's all. It'll pass—the next book I read will be communistic. But it's funny he didn't answer me. Come on, let's have a look at the house."

CHAPTER NINE

ANNE drove on back through the woods to the gates of the Borghese Palace and snapped off the lights. In the moonlight, bright again with the car lights off, they could see quite plainly. Beyond the chained gates the drive lay straight and wide going evenly up the slight rising ground—and suddenly through the trees they saw the gables of York Seat—the broad, clustered chimneys at both ends—the moonlight a sheet of silver on the roof.

"Come on," Mat said.

"I'm not staying here alone—that's sure."

He took her arm and helped her out and they pushed through the undergrowth beside the gates and came into the drive—two dark figures under the trees, their faces white in the moon.

They kept on up the drive to the old carriage oval where it swept around right and left, and they stopped. The house was not a hundred yards from them now, silent and black in the full light of the moon—a forgotten house. Frowning, its hat pulled down in disgust over its heavy-lidded eyes. The main section was three stories high with stone steps leading up from the terraces to the double-doored entrance. It was the roof of that that they had seen from the gates. On either side, wings led out to identical sections at each end. Those sections had the same mild Georgian gable slope, but they were only two stories high.

Mat stood there, head up, looking at it and breathing deeply with a strange emotion. There it is—the whole history of your tribe. Love and wounds and the death of children. Hope and disappointment and fear. Here's the book—with all of it written in. Sickness and death and health and happiness. Triumph and defeat. Glory and the dark well of dishonor. Laughter and tears. Cadet Robert E. Lee tracing his initials on a window-pane with a lady's diamond years before Major Robert E. Lee crossed the Potomac to his beloved Arlington for the last time. Governor Robert Davanan stood at that door when the courier from Baltimore galloped up to bring him word of his election. Admiral Badenoch smoked his churchwarden on that unkempt terrace. The British came up through the woods from their long-boats in the Bligh River in 1812 and politely sacked the house. Mat laughed softly.

"What?"

"I'm laughing," he said, "because I've just realized how much time and effort it takes to make a hundred-dollar-a-week Amalgamated Press man. How do you like my little hideaway on the Eastern Sho'?"

"It's a gorgeous place," Anne breathed. "And it's not spooky at all. It's a kind house just waiting to be treated decently again."

Mat said, "It's got me. I've been here before. I know it. I could live here—I've never felt like that about any other place in my life—"

Her hand on his arm, clutching, stopped him. "Look on the roof—right by the chimneys on the left—" her voice broke.

He looked up quickly. There was a man standing there, full height, right beside the chimneys, his back against them, his head tilted to the sky above, smoking a cigarette.

And that was a most outrageous thing. There is no other word for it but outrageous. He was standing up there in the moonlight, his back against the old chimneys, smoking his cigarette as casually as he'd smoke it in a theater lobby or on a street corner if he were waiting for some one. He was a fairly tall man and slender, and there he stood. And that's all he was doing—standing there, smoking his cigarette. There was no calling to this man. If you called, he'd say "Well?" with a fine insolence. If you asked him who he was, he'd want to know why you wanted to know. And he'd make it plain to you that he had the right to know. Some people you can get like that at a distance. That man you could all right. And don't mistake it.

For a moment Mat couldn't speak. Instinctively, they dodged back into the tree shadows. "No," Mat whispered, "you've made that up!"

"You saw him, too."

"Of course I saw him—but I made it up, too."

"There is a man up there on the roof—smoking a cigarette!" Anne hissed. Mat looked up again. From where they were now, the broad shoulders of the chimneys hid the man. They moved to the right slightly, and crept back to where they had been standing when they first saw him. He was gone.

"Now look here," Mat said. "Did we see a man up there?"

"I did—but where is he?"

"That's just it. So did I. But where is he?"

"Now listen," Anne said, "we both saw him—where's he gone?"

Mat shook his head. "I'm that way now myself. Look at my hand," he held it out. It was shaking.

"Feel mine," she said and she put them in his. They were like two small, wet fish. "We can't both be wrong. We both saw him!"

Mat said: "Ghosts don't smoke cigarettes."

"He wasn't a ghost," Anne shook her head. "There was a man up there on the roof, looking at the moon—smoking a cigarette."

"Well, there doesn't seem to be a policeman in sight. There never is when you want one. So what do we do?"

"I don't know. If he's gone, he's gone down inside the house and I'll tell you frankly I don't like being stared at by people at night—from the windows of very old, dark houses."

"You have a point there. Neither do I, now that you remind me of it."

"So let's go home," she said.

"No," he shook his head. "I've got to walk clear around the house slowly before I go."

"For Heaven's sake—why?"

"Because I'm afraid I'll faint from fright if I do. So I've got to. I'm built that way. I'm a blithering coward. I always have to do everything I'm afraid to do or I'm not happy. Are you coming with me?"

"I can't."

"It'll be worse staying here waiting for me."

"I won't wait—I'll run for the car if you leave me—"

"The hell you will—"

"Don't walk around that house!" she took his arm.

"Why?"

"I don't know why. Just don't!"

He said: "Look here, Anne—you are frightened, aren't you?"

"Desperately—terribly—I can feel cold hands touching my back inside my clothes." He felt her hands shaking in his, heard her teeth chattering—knew that in a second she'd go all to pieces.

"Hold it, Baby," he said sharply. "Nothing's going to happen to you—to any one." And he tightened his fingers on her hands to steady her. The quietness of the place closed in around them sharply as they stood watching the house. Night silence, with a sly breath in the trees and the distant howl of a dog, miles away, and the whisper of a faint breeze in the field grass below like the frou-frou of skirts.

From the direction of the house, there was a sharp crack suddenly, like the sound a board makes when pulled free of a packing-case, and as they turned the front door opened. Anne started to run blindly but Mat caught at her jacket and held onto her. "Quiet!" he hissed. "Stand still—I won't let any one hurt you. It's the man who was on the roof—" He pulled her into the tree shadows and they stood there, their breath in each other's faces, staring back at the house.

Whoever had opened the front door, came out on the stone steps, closed it sharply behind him, tried the knob to see if it was locked and walked easily down the steps to the terrace. He turned the collar of his coat up against the chill of the air, settled his hat brim over his face and, hands in pockets, stepped down into the carriage oval and started walking briskly away from them in the full light of the moon. The wind caught the brown tang of his cigarette, shredded it thinly and tore it across their nostrils. He walked across the oval toward the fields that rolled down to the Wreck Point Road.

Mat stiffened and half opened his mouth to call, but the girl clapped her hand over it, pressing her fingers into his face, clinging to him frantically. "Don't—don't!" And the man was gone in that moment.

"Why not? Why shouldn't I call to him? Whoever he is—he has no right in that house—it's my house, isn't it?"

"Don't you feel it now?"

"What?"

"I don't know," she shivered helplessly, "but something terrible—in the way he was standing there on the roof—in the way he came out and tried the door and walked off across the oval, something not quite—human!"

"No—I'm damned if I did," Mat snorted.

"But there was," she insisted, "something quite frightful in his casualness, I tell you—just as there was in that man at the St. Daviston Hotel." She stopped.

"Go on."

"It was that man!"

"You're going completely screwball now."

"I know it," she covered her face with her hands. "I know it—but I can't help it."

"Well, was it—or wasn't it?"

"No—it couldn't have been."

"Look here—you've had something on your mind ever since Saturday night."

"Please, let's go back to town!"

He snorted. "I've had enough, too," and he took her arm and headed down the drive.

There were clouds coming up from the bay now—a low bank of them. They caught the moon suddenly and smothered it. They groped around the Italian gates and back to the car. Anne said: "Do give me a cigarette—I'm still jittery." In the silence, they heard another car's motor in the direction of Wreck Point Road, across the fields to the right. Lights flashed on over there—a wash of broad headlight beams and the querulous finger of a ditch light that stabbed the trees for a second and melted in with the headlights. Then they moved forward, joggling slowly as if they were on a bad road too. Anne started her own motor and kept parallel to the other lights, her dimmers on. That way they passed between the old gateposts of York Seat and came on out of the Little Creek Road. The other car, slightly ahead of them, got into the Wreck Point Road before they did and turned in the direction of Thorpe's Corners. Just as they came to the Junction of the Little Creek and Wreck Point roads, it snarled furiously past them.

"There must be another road down there that leads in to the house."

"Not to-night," Anne shook her head. "This child goes to bed—with the covers over her head."

CHAPTER TEN

BACK in town, the radio in Applethorp's drug-store was still blaring and it was only nine-thirty by Mat's watch when they garaged the car.

The night policeman was still in the garage, talking with the garageman.

"Find the Little Creek Road?" he asked.

"Yes," Mat called. "Thanks."

Anne and he walked slowly around the corner to the Chincoteague Hotel and up the veranda steps. It was ridiculous, coming back from York this way into the bucolic simplicity of the town. Absurd, suddenly, that there should have been a man on the roof of York Seat. Mat's mind crawled with resentment at it. He was furious about it suddenly.

"Well," he said, "I guess that's the evening."

"Yes," she held out her hand, "good night."

Her eyes were on his evenly and she was herself again after her fright. She said: "Please forget what I did—going to pieces that way. I was terribly upset. I've only lost my head once before in my life, and I'll always be ashamed of that time—"

"And you won't tell?"

"I can't ever." She tightened her fingers on his hand. "Good night." She turned from him and went up the stairs. The lobby was empty and the clerk was not behind his desk. Mat sat down and pulled out a cigarette. The telephone buzzed briefly at the switchboard—and stopped buzzing. The clock across the lobby ticked loudly—forcing itself on the quietness. Outside in the street, a car motor started and somebody called good night.

Whoever had been on the roof of York had been up there waiting for that other car. It must have come in that other road after Mat and Anne were well down the Little Creek Road. Behind them, they wouldn't have seen its lights, and their own lights with the dimmers on were hidden by the trees and the thick growth of the Little Creek Road. They couldn't see the other car's lights walking up the new drive to York Seat either, because they were hidden by the rising ground the house stood on. But the man on the roof could see those lights. That's what he was up there for—waiting for them. Who in hell is it—somebody hiding out in York—getting his food from that other car? Perhaps. With the local haunt legend, that might be quite possible—but it sounds absurd. Absurd or not, what about my great-uncle's death? Anybody hiding out at York Seat comes in for questioning on that—that's certain. He got up and walked to the windows and stood for a moment looking out into the dimly lit street. He heard the clerk come in from the back part of the hotel.

"Well," he said cheerfully, "have a little drive?"

"Yes," Mat said.

He was thinking of Anne now. What's she done that she's ashamed of? He shrugged. She's young enough still to take a lot of things seriously that she wouldn't if she was a little older. Hell—I hope it isn't a man. Jealousy shot through him suddenly like a physical pain. Here, he said to himself, what's this? If it is a man you can't help it, so why get that way about it? And it probably is—so don't get that way. Maybe that's why she's been standoffish. Maybe some swine has smudged her up. That happens.

He turned angrily from the windows, and the dining-room doors opened and Mrs. Vom Bloercke came out. Mat stared at her. She stood there for a moment, her hand on the doorknob, her face quite pale. Seeing her again, he remembered the exquisite breath of her perfume. It was not that it was perfume alone, as it is with some women as make up is—as clothing. It was faint and quietly unobtrusive, a definite part of her, as her eyes were, her lovely hair. She was fresh and beautifully groomed. She wore two pink camellias and he remembered for a second her unreality when he had first seen her. That was gone from her now. She was completely real as she stood there looking at him. An exquisite woman, quite unbelievably beautiful—in the pale impersonal way that marble is beautiful, and he realized suddenly that he had been wrong, when he saw her first, in feeling shocked because that beauty of hers was gone. She smiled suddenly—and it was there, complete and perfect with the warmth of that smile. Not warmth for him—but warmth for some inner amusement she knew and kept quietly to herself.

He said, "Hello—nice to see you again."

"I didn't know you planned to come down so soon."

Her voice was pleasant. There was a softness to the flow of her words that was infinitely soothing.

"I didn't," he said. "I just came, when I found I'd inherited York."

"I see—"

He said: "Have you seen Dr. de Wolff since he talked to me? You see you left me every one's telephone number but your own— your banker wrote and your lawyer—and Dr. de Wolff called on me—"

She said: "He has gone to Europe. He sailed yesterday with a special visa ..." she was embarrassed suddenly, holding her hands with her gloves in them tightly together in front of her, looking up at him earnestly, pleading almost. "He does that at times— all psychoanalysts do," she said. "They leave you for a month or so when the analysis reaches a certain point, so that you do not become too dependent upon them."

"I see." Her words embarrassed him for he felt her strange fear again.

"And I came right down here—driving—by easy stages." She smiled. "You see this is the only part of the world that I feel spiritually at home in—spiritually comfortable in. There is a texture to living here that you can get your fingers into—a warp and woof. You see life in the faces of people, instead of that nervous pursuit of a living that you have in New York. Their voices vibrate with living. They are whole people still, not yet fragmented by civilization—as we are."

He nodded. "I have felt it in the few hours I have been here—the quietude of backwaters."

She shook her head. "Not backwaters, Mr. Davanan. What you feel down here is the even, untrammeled flow of the full tide. New York is the backwater—a distorted rip of whirlpools and eddies and cross currents that give you no peace for living—no time for anything but keeping your head up and fighting to survive."

"You have something there—"

"Ah, yes," she said, "I have. And some day you will acquire it. But not yet. You are not ready for Maryland yet," she smiled, "for you are still a fighting man and New York is the best battle-field in the world. But I don't want battles any longer. I want peace. And I shall have it soon. I felt it come over me as I crossed the Delaware at New Castle yesterday. To-day, driving the rest of the way here—this hotel. I arrived about three-thirty and I've slept like a child until a little while ago. I have become a new woman, strong in my full right once more. Do you," she half reached a hand toward him, "realize what that can mean to some one who nearly lost it?"

There was no desperation in her voice—just a quiet statement of accepted fact. But it was the simplicity of it that got Mat. He stood there in front of her, his hands damp and a racing nerve chill in his lower arms.

He looked at her steadily. "Go on," he said, and he was conscious in that moment of exactly what she did to him—of what that compulsion of hers was. The attraction of all women to all men begins with stimulation of the ego. It makes men feel their power and that feeling is sublime—the artificial ecstasy of drugged emotions. And Madeleine Vom Bloercke could put him almost completely under. Only one small spot of consciousness remained to let him rebel. But he had lived long enough in the world to know that his sanity depended on that spot—to know that the best things of life come in only after ego goes completely—not when it runs amok like a hop-headed gangster.

She was speaking as if to herself. "Most people can say I was born on such a date," she said, "that their father's name and their mother's name were so and so. That they lived in such a place and went to this school and that school. That they fell in love with this man, and to-day that they are this age or that age. That is their birthright. But I never had that." She looked up at him helplessly, her eyes wide, "for I was born in time brackets that I can't define. All that I know about myself is that all of my love and my hope and my guilt was born with me intact and that it has been my job to try, as best I could, to define them for what they were."

She walked slowly toward the veranda doors. He opened them for her and they stepped outside into the cool breath of night.

For a moment he stood there looking at her without speaking. Her emotion had passed from her eyes and she was almost girlish, a slender woman with the same fine grace of womanhood that Anne Langdon had—the grace of breeding, that no surface patina can counterfeit. But there was some quality of agelessness in Mrs. Vom Bloercke—the warmth of inner wisdom perhaps that had not come to Anne Langdon yet. That was her unreality, and for a moment it was frightening. The fiber that made her being was not dated. As she was, as she stood there, her fundamental character would have been adequate, he felt, in any period of history—for any dramatic crisis.

He said: "The reason I mentioned de Wolff is that I told him you might have the house—as soon as I have settled the details."

"Yes," she said, "he told me that before he sailed for Europe. I must thank you," she said and she nodded to him pleasantly, "for all you have done."

She looked at him steadily for a moment, then before he could move if he'd wanted to, she leaned toward him and kissed him on the cheek. He stood there like a goat, his hand half up to his face; then he caught her arm tightly in his fingers. "Just a minute," he said huskily. "What kind of a woman are you?"

Her eyes were clear. "That was not for you," she said. "I don't know what kind of a woman I am. Do you?"

"No—I'm damned if I do, but I'll find out!"

"If you do, you're a fool!"

"No," he shook his head firmly. "Don't say that—it's so easy to call people fools—but why should I be one because you attract me desperately and because I admit it to you? Because when I am with you, I feel a weakness to do for you in every fiber of me—that is the only real strength I have ever known? Please, Madeleine, hear me out to the end; you owe me that. You and I are one of those things that must happen probably—and for me, I am powerless now to stop it. If I hadn't seen you again, it would have passed as an incident, but now that I have seen you again, it can't. Don't move back—" He put both of his hands on her upper arms, flat, and held them there, forcing her gently between his open palms. "Because there are many things that I must know before I leave you to-night."

He saw the light shine briefly on her teeth as she pressed them into her lower lip. She closed her eyes.

"Don't, Matthew."

"Oh, yes," he nodded vigorously, "I will—right here and now. You feel it. You felt it since the moment you stepped into my apartment in New York—and I've felt it."

She put her fingers to his lips. "This is so desperately unfair, my dear, so desperately unfair."

"In God's name, how is it unfair?"

"Not to you," her voice was soft, "but to me." Almost she sobbed, "to me. Do you hear me? This should not have happened. That it has, is one of the cruelest jests of fate."

"Because you feel that you are ill," he asked her, "that you are not capable of meeting it? Madeleine—" He shook her gently and put his face close to hers. She closed her eyes and suddenly in the faint light, he saw that her face was drawn, that she was tired, that there was no strength left in her.

"Madeleine," the fragrance of her was in his brain, "I'm not this Captain Molleston. Look at me, I'm Matthew Davanan. I don't even look like Captain Molleston looked. After you told me I did, I read the book on York Seat—saw his name mentioned and looked his portrait up in Malinoff's book on Sir Henry Raeburn. There isn't the slightest resemblance between me and the portrait of Captain Molleston that hangs in the Tate Gallery."

She didn't answer him for a moment, then she said, "You are very young, Mr. Davanan—very ingenuous." And he felt five years old as she said it—awkward, uncomfortable—three-cornered-pantish.

"Go back to New York—now—" And her arms were around his neck—her face pressed to his, her tears wetting his cheek, and her body clinging so tightly to him that for a moment they were part of each other and in that moment his spot of reality was gone and he was a lost man.

"Madeleine—Madeleine," he whispered.

Years later he would know that what he felt in that moment was the nearest approach to godhood that man is given. That moment in which suddenly the Roman Empire became a handful of dust to be flung aside angrily for the sake of a woman. But even as he felt that brief flash of immortality, the hard-headed centuries of his breeding closed in upon him and left him with the embers of anger burning fiercely in the ashes of his pride while the bitter smoke that is man's heritage of his own shame choked him.

"You will promise me that," she said fiercely, "for you owe it to me. Go back to New York. Leave me here alone for just a short while, to collect myself, and then if I can I will follow you."

"That's utterly ridiculous," he snorted, "why go back to New York?"

"Because I ask you to," she said earnestly. "I ask you to leave me quite alone with this thing you have brought into my life, for a short while until I can overtake myself again."

"I'm not going to—I can't leave you."

"You must."

"No," he said, "and nothing can make me." Then suddenly he saw her tears.

"Don't cry," he said hoarsely, "I can't stand it!"

She let go of him, put her hands on his and stepped back. "Go away now, please. This is quite enough. This is all there is. Go away now or all your life you'll regret it that you didn't!"

"I'm not going."

"Then I am," she said. "No, you mustn't touch me again—ever. You mustn't think of me—but you will, and that's why I called you a fool, Matthew Davanan, for you are a fool—" She held both hands to her eyes for a moment, breathing deeply, trying to control herself. "Oh, why," she said softly, "why?"

"I can't stand it, Madeleine!"

Are you mad yourself, Davanan? What the hell do you know about this woman—about life? You haven't even worn off the gilt of sentiment yet. All you've done for twenty-eight years is to admit you're a male animal and act accordingly. He wanted to dash past her but he felt again that strange compulsion that had come over him at their first meeting—a feeling in him that he had known her much longer than he actually had. She could do that. Frankness, perhaps. Frankness that drew out frankness in him. An ease of manner that put people at ease. She couldn't be more than two or three years older than he was, but that didn't explain her quiet dignity—that dignity was naturalness—a part of the fiber of the woman.

But her dignity was gone now.

"You can't stand it?" she said sharply. "What can't you stand? I can't stand it! Listen to me—" She pressed her hands to her forehead. She had brushed the tears across her cheek and they had wet her hair at the temple, darkening it. "How old do you think I am?"

"I don't care."

"Don't you?" she mocked him. "Well, I'll tell you how old I am and there goes the last breath of decency I ever had—if I ever had any—for years ago there was a boy in my life like you— with eyes like yours and hair with your streak of red in it." She laughed shrilly. "He was your precious Captain Molleston—not a century ago, but almost. I'm tired of life, so I reached out for you in my memory when I met you, but there we end. I am forty-nine years old. My hair is dyed, my body is old and soft with age—that miserable, unhealthy softness that time puts upon it and it's a living history of what my life has been to try to forget what it once was. That's all you are to me, a memory of what might have been—"

"Don't!"

"Yes," she nodded.

He was cold now, all over, and the glaze of fear was in his eyes. For a moment he couldn't move or speak. And in that moment she ran from him, down the veranda, down the steps to the sidewalk and past the corner of the hotel. She was climbing into her car when he reached her.

"I think that what you have told me is a ghastly lie—a lie to disgust me and drive me away from you—to cover some other shame that is in your heart. Please tell me that I am right. Please tell me!"

"Will you go back to New York, if I do? Will you leave me alone now?"

"Yes, I'll do anything you say."

She held out her hand and he took it. "I can't stay here with you," she said, "or near you. I'm going to drive south and drive all night. I can't sleep now anyway. Go back to New York and I'll come to you just as soon as I have all this straightened out in my mind. You promise?"

"Of course," he bowed.

She started the car. She sat there, looking at him for a moment, then slowly she let in the clutch. His impulse was not to follow her—but to stand there feeling the echo of her presence close to him even as the echo of her motor died in the Salisbury Road. Poor, tortured soul! And he wanted to cry for her. What is it that happens to people in life—that had happened to her. The suffering of other people!

The clerk came out as he went back up the veranda steps.

"Friend of yours?" the clerk asked him. Mat stood there, completely off his horse. "Yes," he said and still he stood there. What in hell is the story behind her? She's no screwball—she's in desperate trouble. And what in hell is it she does to me? She pulls me up standing, lashes me to the mast—not as a woman—I mean not as a woman I can do anything about—but as a woman I want to do things for.

The clerk said, "Nice looking. She wanted some supper—but she didn't eat it when I had the cook get it for her. She's driving on."

The hotel clock pointed to ten-thirty. Mat turned back to the lobby chairs to smoke one more cigarette, decided against the clerk's conversation, and went up to his room. Exhaustion flooded through him as he sat on the bed taking off his shoes—the heavy weariness of a long drive in fall air. He got his clothes off somehow, crawled under the covers and snapped out the light. Sleep closed over him like thick liquid and he sank into oblivion, but something bothered his face—wouldn't quite let it alone. He kept turning his head slightly to get away from it—a pipe-stem somebody was trying to get into his mouth and he didn't smoke pipes. It was cold and hard and then amazingly it clicked loudly right in his face, and he came to. There was a scattering rush of soft feet in the darkness of his room—and the closing of his door. He snapped on the light in a complete daze and stared at the empty room, his tongue touching the cold spot on his lips. It was after four by his wrist-watch, and as he pulled up his arm to look at it, something slid off his chest. He reached for it and touched its cold metal.

It was a thirty-eight caliber Colt automatic and the end of the blued steel barrel was iridescent with dark moisture from his mouth. The barrel of that gun had been in his mouth and some one had pulled the trigger—for a misfire. He swung out of bed, trembling and stood there beside it, his breath sucked in tight.

CHAPTER ELEVEN

THE stark horror that held him at the sight of that gun on the bedclothes kept him from moving—but his mind worked inside its coercion—too well. He got it all in a white rush. Some one had crept into his room in the darkness, that gun in hand, and had quietly tried to force the muzzle between his lips— had forced it part way in and pulled the trigger to kill him and make it look like suicide. But the gun had misfired. If the gun had fired he'd be lying there now, cooling—with his astonished eyes popped wide and a great damp hole from the roof of his mouth to the clotting hairs on top of his head. And there would be feet pounding wildly on the stairs—in the corridors of the old hotel—slippered feet, racing in fear toward the sound of the shot—faces at his open door, white with terror, his light punched on and people staring at the young man in Room 20 who had seemed all right early in the evening but who had gone upstairs and gone to bed and calmly put a gun in his mouth and killed himself. Why?

He could see himself covering his own suicide. Young reporter. Girl? Mebbe. You never knew about the girl angle. Girls got some people that way. Money? Hell, no. He had a good job. Besides, he'd just come into York Seat from his great-uncle's will. Hold it—first Charles Davanan—now you, you fool! That's it.

He shot the bolt on his door. The room was bitter cold. He got back into bed and reached for the gun, but stopped his hand half way to it, covered it with the edge of the sheet and threw the hanger back. The shell in the chamber sprang out at him and the action of the gun clicked loudly in the silence. The cap of that shell was scored where the firing pin had hit it. Some workman in Hartford, Connecticut—or Chicago or Wilmington, Delaware, hadn't loaded that cap quite to specifications. Slovenly, and because of it, Mat Davanan was still alive. Or the cartridge was old. How old did a cartridge have to be to misfire? Would just one extra day of age do it? Or the firing pin of the gun was worn. How many times did a gun have to be fired to wear the pin just enough to cause it to misfire? Would one extra pulling of the trigger do it? Would it fire on the 4000th try but not on the 4001st?

Stop this. The point is who wants to get rid of you—not why they failed. Your great-uncle comes back from Europe, and comes over here from Baltimore and gets himself killed. You come down here and somebody tries to get you the first night. Who knows about both of you? Miers Buckmaster? You went to bed at ten-fifteen—six hours or more ago. In six hours Buckmaster could walk into town on his hands and knees.

All right. Who else? The man on the roof of York Seat? He's suspect as hell for just being there—but how does he know about me? Hold it. My name is on this hotel register. Anybody could see it there who happened to look—or be watching for it. Seeing it—they could drive out to York and tell that man and he could drive back with them and sneak in to do the job. That would explain that other car we saw down there. Or would it? Maybe that other car belonged to the man on the roof. Maybe he drove there in it and drove away in it. There doesn't have to have been any one else in it. But suppose there was. Who knows me here—knows that I am here?

Lord Innes, Anne, and Mrs. Vom Bloercke. Lord Innes and Anne are as straight and open-faced as any two people could be. Mrs. Vom Bloercke tells me to go back to New York. She is a self-admitted screwball but the Seaforth National vouches for her. Dr. de Wolff vouches for her, and her lawyer Upjohn vouches for her. You can't deny references like that no matter what, and she didn't know I would be down here so soon. She was surprised at seeing me in the lobby.

But this is no story I'm on. This is me. Somebody's trying to kill me—and they are trying to kill me because I've come into York Seat. The main point, my boy, is that somebody has tried, but they haven't tried in the open because they want an alibi. If Andrew Goldsboro is right about my uncle—they got an alibi there and they tried to with me—because they don't want a murder investigation. This is the last night you spend in this hotel—or anywhere near it.

Mat got up and started to dress feverishly. He tied his tie, wrapped the gun in a handkerchief and slipped it in his right-hand jacket pocket, on the off chance that it might have fingerprints on it even though it is a matter of record in New York City that only five murder guns in twenty years have had fingerprints on them, because the way the hand holds a gun just doesn't put prints on it. It was almost six by his watch, but it was still dark outside when he snapped off his light. He opened his door quietly and looked out into the silent hall. Then he stepped out, locked the door and went down into the deserted lobby.

Somebody was yawning noisily behind the desk—somebody he couldn't see. He went across, leaned over and looked down. The same clerk was there, lying on an army cot behind, with his shoes and coat off.

"Hello—up early, aren't you?"

"Yes," Mat said, "can't sleep in the morning."

"How about some coffee?"—the clerk got up and stretched. Mat pulled the register around and looked at the last open page. There they were—the three of them. Mr. Montgomery, Anne Langdon, and Matthew Davanan. Madeleine Vom Bloercke hadn't registered.

"Don't do much business here, do you?"

"Not much—you three are the only people staying here. Those two salesmen last night went on to the Wicomico in Salisbury."

"Listen," Mat said, "and don't get excited. Are there back stairs to this hotel?"

"Yeah—sure."

"Another street door besides this one?"

"Yep—around the side."

"Either of 'em locked?"

"Nope—no need to lock anything in this town."

"I see."

"Why—what's up?"

"Nothing. Let me ask you another question. Mr. Montgomery been downstairs?"

"Ain't seen him since last night."

"The girl with him—Miss Langdon?"

"Ain't seen her since she came in with you last night and went upstairs."

"Mrs. Vom Bloercke came back—after I talked to her on the veranda?"

"Nope. Why?"

"Nothing."

Mat went out on the veranda. He stood there for a moment. All right. Steady. Think it out. He went down the veranda stairs. He crossed the street and stood for a moment looking at the Confederate Memorial in the park. He walked over casually and read the names on it to steady himself: Durburrow, Caton, Irons, Sykes, Mifflin, Crapper, Chest, Tilghman, Laws, Ewbanks, Covington, Manlove—the old yeoman fabric that once was America—dead these seventy-odd years at Table Mountain, the Wilderness and the Peninsula. Lee's ragged minstrels. He walked on around Court House Square, looking up at the blank brick faces of the silent buildings. "Andrew Caton, Attorney-at-Law"— "Lester Ewbanks, Hay, Grain and Feed." Some of the old blood still left, crusted and dried out.

The day was in its first clear whiteness now—that still white light of early morning when the outlines of walls are sharp and the grating of crisp leaves in gutters is the only live thing in a dead world. Court House Square was suddenly an entirely artificial structure, put up consciously on a studio lot—complete in every detail—waiting for camera crews and extras. Mat walked on around to the Court House at the end, past "A. Gold, Cleaning and Pressing," and started up the north side. Ahead of him, there was a farm truck at the curb, and a sign on the building beside it swinging from iron brackets "Talbot Pyle—Attorney-at-Law." A window on the second floor above the sign, was lighted still against the vanished darkness. "Talbot Pyle, Attorney-at-Law." He had the momentary feeling that Mr. Pyle was denying the doubt in his mind that he was an attorney by the simple process of putting up as many signs to that effect as he could find room for on his premises.

Mat pushed open the street door and looked in the dusty vestibule. There was a sign in there with an arrow pointing to the stairs: "Talbot Pyle, Lawyer." Mat went slowly up the creaking stairs to the landing above. There was one door up there with a band of light under it, and "Talbot Pyle—Attorney-at-Law" across it. He knocked. There was a grating of chair legs on the bare floor inside, a cough and a man's voice; "Who is it?"

Mat opened the door. Miers Buckmaster, in a long bearskin overcoat, sat in a low-backed arm-chair tilted against the wall. His overall pants were stuffed into the tops of buckled arctics and he held an ear-tabbed shooting cap in his hands. The man behind the desk was a most surprising incongruity in that littered office.

"Mr. Pyle?—I'm Matthew Davanan."

Mr. Pyle was a travesty of metropolitan legal success. His suit was a cheap pepper-and-salt mail order shoddy, but pressed to razor-edged creases. His narrow shoes were brilliantly shined. He wore a clean, starched wing-collar with a blue and white polka-dot bat's-wing tie—and his cuffs at his thin wrists were heavy and studded with onyx and gold links as large as quarters. But the most amazing thing about him was his head. It was one of those racially old heads, painfully high and narrow and well-rounded. The head of an important, successful man. You felt that years ago, Talbot Pyle had recognized the possibilities in the physical contours of his head and had conformed his entire life to it. It was the head of an eminent surgeon—of the Chairman of the Military Affairs Committee—of the Ambassador to St. James's—stuck blindly on a six-hundred-dollar-a-year States Attorney on the Eastern Shore of Maryland. He wore pince-nez on a black ribbon—two polished discs of crystal to protect his anemic eyes from the world. Eyeglasses on some people always look frozen. Talbot Pyle's looked frozen.

He stared at Mat, vacantly. Mat said, "I came down unexpectedly last night from New York."

"You did?" Pyle said.

"You know who I am, don't you?"

Buckmaster was staring at him, that blank look of the country man waiting to be convinced but not believing for a minute that he is going to be.

"Wait a minute," Pyle said. "I had a letter here from Mr. Andrew Goldsboro. Just a couple of days after Mr. Charles Davanan's death." He swiveled around to his old pine letter file behind him, opened it and started to riffle through it. "Yes, sir," he drew out a letter and spread it in his hands. "Here it is. Mr. Matthew Davanan. Now you must be that Mr. Matthew Davanan, last known to be residing in New York City?"

"I must be," Mat said coldly.

Pyle's mouth spread into a thin-lipped smile.

"Well, then, sir—you're Mr. Charles Davanan's grand-nephew."

"I can assure you that I am."

"Well, now, Mr. Davanan, I'm right glad to meet you. Right glad." Pyle stood up briskly and came out from behind his desk, his hand held out. The fact that it was seven o'clock made no difference to him.

"Good morning," Mat said. "Morning, Buckmaster." Miers Buckmaster nodded in evident relief.

Pyle said, "Buckmaster told me somebody'd been down to see him last night—that must have been you."

"That's not what I came here for," Buckmaster said evenly.

"No—it's not," Pyle nodded and pulled a chair. "Sit down, Mr. Davanan. We've got a problem here you ought to be in on. Suppose you tell Mr. Davanan what you've told me, Buckmaster."

Miers Buckmaster shifted his quid to his left cheek. "It's about the Government man," he said, "this fella, Tom Carter."

"What do you mean—a Government man?"

"It's this way," Buckmaster said, "them oyster beds off the mouth of the Bligh River—straight acrost from Wreck Point to Lloyd Light—have been closed for seeding by the Government. They ain't nobody supposed to tong there until they're opened again. But they been tonging at night and the Government got wind of it and sent this Tom Carter over here about a month ago to catch whoever was poaching on those beds. He was around Thorpe's Corners a couple days before he came down to see me. He told me who he was and asked me to keep it quiet. Nice fella, Tom Carter. He told me who he was because he wanted me to give him a line on the Bligh River fishermen. Well, I seen him around for about a week after that, then he disappeared. Only I guess maybe he didn't."

"What did he do?"

"I don't rightly know," Miers said, "but I got my suspicions, so I come in to tell Mister Pyle."

"Tell Mr. Davanan, Miers," Pyle said.

Miers Buckmaster moved heavily in his chair. "Well, my old woman is sort of soft on York Seat, Mister Davanan. Goes up and dusts around the house every day or so. She can't keep it clean, but she sort of keeps an eye on it and since Mr. Charles' funeral, she puts flowers on his grave when she goes up, if they're any flowers growing handy. You know how women are. Well, she went up yesterday morning and in the dining-room of the house, there was a chair broken to bits and a lot of burnt cloth in the dining-room fireplace—a heap of it—and a pair of burnt shoes— and this here on the floor." Miers put his gnarled hand to Talbot Pyle's desk and picked up a brass cartridge case from a crumpled piece of newspaper.

"Let's see it."

Miers handed it to Mat. "And that ain't all," he said. "Somebody'd been at Mr. Charles Davanan's grave."

"What do you mean?"

"The sods'd all been fresh cut again and there was dirt sprinkled through the grass all around."

Mat looked at the cartridge case. It was thirty-eight caliber.

"Go on," Mat said.

"That's all," Miers said, "except the burnt shoes. There they are." He nodded to a piece of newspaper on the floor beside his chair. "I brought 'em in for Mr. Pyle to look at." Mat leaned over and looked. There wasn't much left of the shoes except the charred soles and heels, heavily studded with calks.

"They're my shoes," Miers said. "I lent 'em to Carter one day he got his feet wet trampin' through the swamp land between my place and Wreck Point."

"What do you think, Mr. Davanan?" Talbot Pyle clasped his hands and leaned on his desk.

"I don't know," Mat said.

Miers Buckmaster stood up and gathered his bearskin coat about him. "Only thing is—if anything happens to a Government man—there'll be another one along to find out about it, so I come in to tell Mister Pyle first."

"Sit down a minute," Mat said. "Tell me about the house."

"Tell you what about it?"

"Well, for instance. I don't suppose anybody would go there without your knowing something about them?"

"Hardly," Buckmaster said. "People come by at times, but more in the summer than now—to see the place, as you might say, because it's sort of historic. Once in a while you get somebody who says their ancestors lived there. That sort of thing. Sometimes in the summer an archytect'll come by—or a painter to look it over and make drawings. Sometimes at night you see a car going in the drive for a little lovemaking mebbe."

"I see—anybody been by lately?"

"Nope—only you."

"There was a man in the house last night," Mat said.

"Who?"

"I don't know."

"How do you know then?" Buckmaster looked startled.

"I went up the drive and I saw him in the moonlight, standing on the roof smoking a cigarette. Five minutes later he came out the front door and walked across the fields toward Wreck Point Road."

"Who was it?"

"I don't know."

"Now wait a minute," Buckmaster said, "that can't be. It don't make sense."

"I can't help that. He was there."

"That's an old house, Mister Davanan."

"What's that got to do with it?"

"Well—I don't know. Old houses you know. When I was a boy I heard grown men swear by the Bible they'd seen old Dandy Davanan riding up the drive on his horse—riding in the front door and up the stairs. Heard his horse's hoofs going up the stairs and into his bedroom—and the date on his tombstone is 1761."

"No," Mat shook his head, "you can't tell me that in broad daylight. Come around after nightfall, Buckmaster."

"Now, Mister Davanan—I ain't saying I believe sech sto-ries—or even about the ha'nt I told you of last night. But there's people that do—and they do say some people are more that way than other people."

"This man was alive. He was smoking a cigarette."

"But it still don't make sense." Buckmaster looked quickly at Talbot Pyle. "Does it, Mister Pyle?"

Pyle cleared his throat, "Well, I don't know."

"I mean," Buckmaster said, "what would any one be standing on the roof for? In the house—yes. Mebbe to steal some of the stuff. But not on the roof. That's not sensible."

"What's in it to steal?" Mat asked him.

"Well, there's all the old stuff. But we ain't ever had any trou-ble about it because the niggers are the ones to steal down here and they're afraid of the house—"

"What old stuff?"

"It's all furnished still—and my wife says a lot of the fur-niture is that antique stuff some people like. She sees pictures in the magazines now and then, like the stuff at the house. One chair I remember that was a thousand dollars. And there's some pictures. Oil-painting pictures—"

"That might be it," Mat nodded, "that may be what that man wants."

Buckmaster shrugged.

"You still think I didn't see him, don't you?"

"I don't know," Buckmaster said. "It don't make much sense though—standing on the roof. If he wanted the stuff that's there, whyn't he take it and go?"

Mat laughed. "All right, Buckmaster. Have you got some time to-day?"

"I'll make time, Mister Davanan. I come into town to get my eggs off on the up train and to get my new separator discs—but I'll be going back out in about an hour and a half."

Mat said, "I'll go out with you. I want to go through that house from top to bottom—and the boat-house, too—"

"There ain't no keys to the boat-house. Ain't ever been in my time."

Talbot Pyle leaned forward.

"There's nothing in the boat-house worth stealing, Mr. Davanan—nothing but the boat."

"Well, I want to see the boat. I've had an offer for it."

"That's the old boat," Pyle said.

"Yes—that's what I thought."

"It's been there as long as I can remember," Pyle said. "It must be pretty much rusted up by now."

"Do you ever remember the boat-house being open?"

"No. The story they tell is that Mr. Charles had a fight with his wife about that boat years ago. It was her father's. They came across the Atlantic in her and Mr. Charles was so seasick he had to go to the hospital in Baltimore. He swore he'd sell the boat and his wife swore he wouldn't sell it. So they compromised. There was always a stone boat-house there and Mr. Charles had it built onto until it was big enough to take the yacht and he had the bar at the mouth of the river dredged, and the yacht hauled in and locked in. He had the windows blocked up and the keys thrown away—so he would never see that yacht again. They say he was just like a woman about things like that—sort of stubborn and outrageous but determined."

Mat laughed. "I see. Well, I'm going in that boat-house. Can you open it, Buckmaster?"

Miers shrugged. "I'll try." He looked troubled. "Likely it'll take dynamite. Them doors is oak and iron-studded and they been tight shut for years, locked and swollen with dampness—"

"As soon as you're ready," Mat said.

"I'll be here." Buckmaster got up and hooked the frogs of his bearskin coat. "I'll leave these things with you, Mister Pyle." He nodded to the cartridge and the burnt shoes.

"Good."

Buckmaster went out and thumped down the stairs and in a moment they heard his motor start and his truck growl off around Court House Square.

CHAPTER TWELVE

"Y OU start the day early," Mat said.

Talbot Pyle coughed behind his hand.

"I live here," he said, "behind the office. Since Mrs. Pyle's death. Miers called me and told me he was coming in early this morning on something important."

"Oh—I see. He called you last night."

"He called about five o'clock yesterday afternoon."

"Now look, Mr. Pyle, I want to talk to you about a few things before Buckmaster gets back. Was there any suspicion of foul play in my great-uncle's death?"

Pyle took off his glasses and wiped them carefully. His eyes without them were like small blue oysters in their own liquor. He wiped his eyes and put the glasses on again. "To be frank," he said judicially, "I think there was a slight suspicion in our minds. But again there's just as good a chance it was an accident."

"Where'd they find his body?"

"They didn't find it right away," Pyle said. "Dr. Sevenoaks said he'd been dead about five days when they found it."

"Where?"

"In the old duck blind off Wreck Point."

"Who found it?"

"Miers Buckmaster."

"Miers Buckmaster? How'd he happen to find it? I mean— did he think something had happened to Charles Davanan? Was he looking for him?"

"No. Miers just went out to shoot."

"I see. How was the body dressed?"

"Sweaters and a shooting coat and pants."

"Just as he would have dressed to shoot duck?"

"Oh, yes—except the hat."

"What kind of hat did he have on?"

"He didn't have any. We didn't find a hat anywhere. That sort of bothered Dr. Sevenoaks and me because it isn't likely a man'd go out in a duck blind bareheaded, is it?"

"No—too cold."

"Yes. Then, again—the hat might have floated away."

"But the wound was all right—that could have been accidental?"

"Yes." Pyle nodded. "All up the side of his neck and his head. Pretty nasty I can tell you—and one shell empty in his gun."

"How long had Charles Davanan been around—before Miers found his body?"

"He'd come here about a week before. He suddenly showed up here one day. Miers didn't know him from Adam. I remembered him vaguely. Miers and I took him to York Seat and he just went through the house once—went through all the lower rooms with us like a man seeing the sights—or something he'd come back to see from childhood memory. Didn't say much or give any orders about the place. We all came out and locked the house up again and Mr. Charles gave the keys back to Miers. Said he'd get the five o'clock bus on Wreck Point Road for the afternoon ferry to Annapolis and we left him walking in the old boxwood gardens, smoking a cigar just as if he still lived there and had come out in the garden for a smoke."

"In other words, he'd come over from Baltimore for just that one day and was going back that night?"

"Yes, that's what he said."

"Well—on the face of it—without baggage, or anything, didn't it strike you as odd when you found him dead a week later in other clothes—with a duck gun in his hand?"

"No," Pyle said, "not very. We just figured he'd seen duck the day he was here so he'd gone back to Baltimore to get his things and come over for a day's shooting. It was his place. He had the right to, if he wanted to."

"And he had no car—or no servant or anybody with him?"

"Nobody. He was a strange man, Mr. Davanan. Anybody'll tell you that who remembers him. Difficult. He didn't talk much and he was sort of arrogant with people. Nobody liked him. He had a short way with his manners. A bedamned-to-you air about him. Lord of the Manor. Well, when people are like that down here, they're left alone pretty much."

"But he was an old man. Too old for duck shooting."

"Nobody's too old for that," Pyle said. "And, besides, Charles Davanan didn't look old. He was tall, and straight, and well preserved."

The telephone rang. He picked up the receiver. "Talbot Pyle's office. Yes, yes, indeed.... Right here in my office. It's for you, Mr. Davanan," and he handed the instrument to Mat.

"For me? Nobody knows I'm here—how can it be for me?" He said "Yes" into the telephone, "Yes, this is Matthew Davanan."

It was the local operator.

"There's a New York call for you. You're staying at the hotel, aren't you?"

"Yes."

"Operator 62. Hold on and I'll see if I can get it for you."

"Do that."

Mat waited. Pyle sat there across the desk, drumming on it nervously, his eyes blinking behind his glasses.

"Wait a minute, Operator. How'd you know I was in Talbot Pyle's office?"

"That's easy, sir. I called the hotel and John Poole said he'd seen you walk around the Square and go into Mr. Pyle's. He's the clerk."

"I get it," Mat said and he had that uncomfortable goldfish feeling suddenly that everybody in town knew as much about his business as he did himself. Small towns are like that. He sat there. There isn't anybody in New York who knows I'm down here on the Eastern Shore except Tommy Powell. That call has got to be Tommy. What's he want?

There was the network clicking out northward in his ear for a moment—up through Wilmington and across the bay, leaping New Jersey into New York, and Tommy Powell's voice was right there in Talbot Pyle's little country law office.

"Hello—Mat? Are you all right?"

"Sure—why?"

"No reason except that I've tried every hotel in every town on the Eastern Shore of Maryland since ten o'clock last night—to find you—"

"What in hell for?"

"You'll find out, boy. Can you take it? Take it then. Here it is. The fingerprints on the foot of the bed in the St. Daviston Hotel, and the fingerprints on our desk are the same man."

"Who is he?"

"The F.B.I. in Washington identifies him as English Frankie Crimmins—a con-man and a high-class international thief, who works with a female front."

"Go on."

"Ready?"

"Yes."

"That girl with you, Anne Langdon—"

"What about her?" Mat said slowly.

"Almost everything," Tommy said. "There's nobody named Langdon in *Who's Who in Art.* The Metropolitan never heard of an American artist of any rank named Langdon—and they haven't any Langdon canvases—and the Bureau of Motor Vehicles never issued a license to an Anne Langdon—"

"So you're still on that—"

"Wait, boy. I know who she is. I checked her with pictures in our morgue. She's Anne Layton. Mixed up with the Tony Hutchinson shooting on Long Island a year ago—a mystery woman in the case, that they never turned up."

For a moment Mat couldn't speak.

"Can you still take it?"

"Go on."

"Lord Innes next," Tommy said. "When I found the girl was a phony I made a quick check on the old man with the British Consulate General. Offhand they didn't place him. Suggested Lord Innes-Vey, an Air Vice-Marshal—but he's in London. So I got me a copy of Burke's Peerage and there is no Lord Innes listed. That'll learn you not to try to learn your grandmother to suck eggs."

Mat said, "Well, who is he?"

"If I wrote mystery stories," Tommy said, "I'd make a guess and say he was English Frankie Crimmins, that he put those prints on his own bed to cover his breaking in on us, for whatever he broke in for. Mind your hind leg, boy, and don't let 'em sell you the Delaware Ship Canal, because I own it and it's not for sale."

When Mat hung up he had a definite mental impulse to be sick to his stomach. There it was still, echoing from the silent telephone. There it was in Tommy's voice and when Tommy went to town on a check-up, he went to town. No going to the zoo with a friend from Cincinnati in this. This was Powell running a story down and hitting it.

Innes is English Frankie Crimmins and Anne is his female front. They've both worked up this Napoleon's bones gag on me with the cleverness of the master crooks they are. While Innes was supposed to be in Washington he must have come over here, when Charles Davanan was here. Charles Davanan got onto what he wanted at York and Innes killed him. Then I inherit York and they find that out. Whatever they want there—it will take time to get. They came to New York. Innes writes me for access to York legitimately, which is their first approach. Anne shadows me to the New York Public Library. All the time Innes was supposed to be sick at the St. Daviston, he must have been actually down here again. That trip, Tom Carter, this Government Fisheries man, interferes with him and he kills Tom Carter. Then he returns to New York after Anne has the stage set for me to meet him. He meets me, and tells me his story. I fall for it and arrange to drive them down here.

So far so good. Now what about the guy who broke in on them at the St. Daviston that night? Either he's somebody on their trail or—No! Mat snapped his fingers. Nobody broke in on them! Those prints were English Frankie Crimmins' prints. Tommy just said so. Innes broke in on himself! They stage it for me to make it look like a third party so that it will be covered up beautifully when Innes breaks in on me the next day in New York. I'm the fly in his ointment since I inherited York Seat. He does that to kill me there—but the cleaning woman gums up those plans by seeing him in my apartment. So then the only course open is for them to come down here with me yesterday and try to get me here. As soon as Innes gets here he plays sick again and behind the alibi of being confined to his room—somehow he goes to York Seat. I surprise Anne into getting her to go out there last night. When we see Innes on the roof, she blows up and won't let me call to him, for fear of my getting on to the whole show. We come back to the hotel and Innes tries to get me in bed and the gun misfires. But what the hell do they want—and whatever it is they'll move fast from now on. They'll have to—because of not killing me last night!

"Bad news?" Pyle asked.

Mat couldn't answer him. All he could see as he sat there was that girl—young and cleareyed and fun. Too young and decent for anything messy like this. It tore at him. She can't be more than twenty-four, and she's got everything that most girls of her age haven't got—an open-faced manner and an honest enthusiasm for life. But she's a liar on all counts and she's in with a crook. What in God's name made her do it? The fool! She had everything.

He heard Buckmaster's truck below the windows and he went out and down the stairs. He got up in the truck's cab and sat down beside Buckmaster and in a few moments they were out Queen Anne Street and across the bridge.

CHAPTER THIRTEEN

CLOSE to, the aroma of Miers Buckmaster was honest but overpowering. It consisted of half a dozen separate factors which were sometimes distinguishable, but which lost themselves in the blending so successfully that in order to separate them into their components of dried perspiration, warm but rather old bearskin, chewing tobacco, oiled leather, horses, and yellow kitchen soap, it was necessary to concentrate intently. They were Buckmaster's life in the living. A more accurate biography of the man would be impossible. He left his life openly before the world, wherever he went. Buckmaster was of the soil. Beyond the things of the soil, his mind was not stimulated.

The girl hung in Mat's consciousness all the way out to Thorpe's Corners—hung there damply in complete disillusion like a ghastly mutilation.

And all the way out, Buckmaster talked heavily. "What we do generally is rotate the River fields and the North Hundred in wheat and field corn and alfalfa, but the Bligh woods ought to go, Mister Davanan. The old growth has been so heavy for years that the new growth hasn't had a chance. I've cruised it and I'd like to take out all the black walnut for milling. There's enough in it to pay for it and the stumping besides, and it'd give York another thirty acres—toward the Point. Now if you'd care to put a little money into it—say about seven hundred dollars—we could drain the swamp between, run it off into Bligh Creek with one retaining wall and we'd have almost a hundred acres additional when we got finished."

Mat said, "I'll look it over."

"You plan to live at York Seat?"

"I don't know," Mat said. "I've got a job in New York and I don't know whether I could fit into the country down here. It can be pretty lonely, I guess."

"Well, I guess any place is if you don't work. And even if you do—a man's got to have a woman. They're botherations—but they sort of pretty up a man's life. That wasn't your wife with you last night by any chance?"

"No," Mat said slowly. "Not by any chance." He lit a cigarette and looked at Buckmaster sideways.

What's this yokel know? A lot he's not talking about. Is he in it? He gives me the haunt nonsense. He wouldn't take me up to York Seat last night. He finds Charles Davanan's body and brings it in. And he tries to tell me I didn't see a man on the roof last night—but he doesn't know about the Government Fisheries man—for he comes in and reports that. Or does he just come in and report it because that'll clear his own skirts if anything's found out?

The truck rattled through Thorpe's Corners. The little crossroads was coming alive with the morning. Alive as it ever was. Canby's store was open and the post-office opposite was open. It was not quite nine o'clock yet. Buckmaster drove on doggedly, past the Little Creek Road Mat and Anne had taken the night before—past the Big Creek Road, his own entrance, and on out toward Wreck Point. He was going to take the back road in to the house, the one the other car had taken the night before.

"Quaint name, Wreck Point," Mat said.

"Nothing quaint about it I can see," Buckmaster said, "couldn't call it anything else. Been too many wrecks on it."

"Yes, I read about it in the book on York Seat."

"Ain't never seen the book," Buckmaster said.

"It was named after the wreck of the ship *Mary and Anne*. Sixteen something."

"Was it now? That's pretty far back."

"Everything's pretty far back down here."

"I guess that's so. But that ain't the only wreck. I can remember half a dozen in my time," Buckmaster said. "The main channel up the Bay from Cape Charles to Baltimore runs close to Lloyd Light and swings in toward Wreck Point and the water this side of it is deep water. If there's fog and a boat misses the turn on the Wreck Point buoy, she'll go straight onto the Cows and Chickens and strike, sure as you're born. The Bay pilots don't like it much in bad weather. I remember a bugeye, when I was a boy, go on in broad daylight. That was kind of awful I'll tell you. She was standing in, all sails set and when she hit, the sticks snapped clean out of her. She went down with all her crew. Make you want to sit right down on the beach and bawl," Buckmaster said. "Yes, sir, cry your heart right out. It's worse seeing a ship die than it is finding her dead people afterwards. I found all three of the bugeye's people. First time I ever seen a dead woman—" he wiped his hand across a tobacco trickle at the corner of his mouth and smeared it into the stubble on his cheek. "Bloat wors'n men they do. Skipper's wife, she were." He shook his head. "Women don't take to drownin' nicely."

The truck flashed past a break in the fence where the bars were down and tracks led in toward York Seat. He hadn't missed the back entrance because he was talking, he'd passed it deliberately.

"Then there was a big steam yacht went on in nineteen sixteen. Belonged to a rich Yankee named Bartholomew. That's when the Government put the Wreck Point gas-buoy in."

Buckmaster kept right on down the Point, rattling his truck on out to the end of the road.

"Now over there to the right, Mister Davanan, is the Bligh woods. You can get an idea of what I'm talking about in just a minute." The road turned sharply right and climbed a slight rise, and then the waters of Chesapeake Bay fanned out suddenly and lay bright for a moment in a brief flash of morning sun. Buckmaster stopped the truck. "That open space ahead is the mouth of the Bligh River," he said, "and all this growth to the right and behind is the Bligh woods. Take it all out and drain the lowland behind my farm and we'd have better than a hundred acres."

"Yes," Mat nodded. "Sounds sensible to me. York Seat," he pointed off to the right, "can't be more than half a mile through those woods—and with the trees out, the back of the house would have the full sweep of the Bay for a view."

"That's right. 'Course we could leave some of the trees close in to the orangery for wind protection—but it'd be an improvement all right."

Mat sat for a moment looking down the rock slope of Wreck Point. It stretched out like a gnarled finger to the rank grass of the water's edge and from the tip of it as far as he could see in the direction of Lloyd Light; the line that hid the sharp rock teeth of the Cows and Chickens was traced across the waters roughly like blue paint spread with a palette-knife. Far out beyond there was the black dot of a buoy.

"That's Wreck Point buoy," Buckmaster said, and he pointed to another dot to the left of the point, "that's the duck blind where Mister Charles was when I found him."

"I see."

Buckmaster backed the truck and turned it and drove back toward the Big Creek Road. And suddenly Mat got it. The man was stalling for time for something. It had taken them at least a half hour longer to come all the way out to Wreck Point—a half hour that might be damned valuable to somebody who needed a half hour for something. That's what all the fancy talk was about—to suck in his interest. He was furious.

"You know, Buckmaster," he said, "you and I aren't going to get along worth a damn."

"Nope, Mr. Davanan, we ain't. And that's a fact. Pity, too, because I'm as good a farmer as you can git—and I put in a lot a sweat in York."

There was a mist veil in the tree tops now and the oppressive weight of rain to come. Fog was rolling in from the Bay, one of those wet Chesapeake fogs that rot your boots and hang in the nostrils like damp wood smoke.

Buckmaster drove on slowly through it, turned in at the Big Creek Road and went on down and into his own stable yard.

"Best we don't part company too hastily, though, Mr. Davanan," he said heavily as he set the brake. "Best we be sure, before we do," and he got out.

There was a woman in a gray Mother Hubbard in the house-yard. She had an enameled basin in her hands. Mat took it for granted she was Miers' wife.

"Mrs. Buckmaster?" he climbed out and walked toward her. "I'm Matthew Davanan. I want to thank you for looking after my uncle's grave."

"Oh, shucks," she said, "that's only decent."

"And the house," he said.

"You going to live there?" she barked at him. The sudden harshness of her voice startled him.

"I don't know," he said.

"Ain't fit to live in."

"Why not?"

"Too big—cold in winter—drafty," and she turned her back and left him standing there feeling about as foolish as he'd ever felt in his life.

There was a clank behind him and he turned in time to see Buckmaster throw a pick and shovel into the back of the truck.

"That's the way she is," Buckmaster said. "Jealous of that house." He spat a flat brown ribbon of tobacco juice at the truck's rear wheel and went back into the barn. Mat got into the truck again and after a moment Buckmaster climbed up with him. This time he had an old Parker gun in his hand.

"If there's anybody hanging around York—this'll ask him why." He put the gun on the seat behind them and drove out to Wreck Point Road.

He turned left in Wreck Point Road—away from the Little Creek Road that Mat and Anne had gone in on last night. "We'll go in the back way," he said. And a moment or two later he turned the truck in toward York Seat on two wagon tracks that led off across the fields.

"Take it easy," Mat said, "this is the road that other car took last night. If the ground gets soft, I want to get out and look for tire tracks."

The fog was down so thickly now that in the hollows they had a visibility of about a hundred and fifty feet only—a white, opalescent fog that cut the tree boles half way up so that the woods to the right looked as if they had been pollarded by shell-fire, the smoke of which still hung above the land. A moment later Buckmaster stopped to get out and open a fence and Mat got out with him.

"This is about where that car stood when its lights went on." Buckmaster pointed to the grass.

"Right there, I guess," he said. The grass was down in two narrow parallel swathes and the grass between them was flecked with black oil. Mat walked around the spot, but that's all there was. "That's the place," he said. "That car didn't go any farther in." Buckmaster had the fence bars down and was stalking back to the truck. "You could see the roof of York from here if it wasn't for the fog." He started the truck and went up the rise through the fence opening. "There you are," he pointed. Mat craned his neck and saw the banked chimneys of the house above the fog wisps on the trees ahead. Anybody standing up there on the roof beside them could see car lights down there in the hollow with no effort. Buckmaster ground the truck up the road in first and a few minutes later they were running along beside the old box gardens and the whole house lay before them, foreshortened from the left wing. The road they were on led up in back across what had once been lawn and passed between the covered washing terrace with its deep-ditched slave prison at one end, and the summer kitchen with its covered passage to the house at the other. To the right, the house walls with the back verandas towered up against the morning sky like an etching run off from an old plate. The thick English ivy had run wild with the years, furring the walls heavily and when Buckmaster shut off the motor, the long lines of windows rattled like old lady's talk. The silence, with that window rattle worrying it slightly, was the silence of death. But the house was not dead, for he had no instinct to shy from it. It was as Anne had said last night—neglected and unkempt, like an old dog without an owner, but it was a pleasant house—waiting patiently to come alive again, waiting to open its eyes and smile again.

Buckmaster stopped the truck and they got out.

"Beyond there," he said, "is what my old woman says they called the Bowling Green." He pointed into the fog. "And way beyond that is the orangery. The graveyard is behind it." Mat nodded, and hands in pockets walked around the east wing to the carriage oval in front. The silence of the house came down on him heavily until he had no talk left in him.

Buckmaster walked across the terrace, trailing his shotgun and went up the steps to the front doors. He put the key in the door, turned it and the great hall of York was open before them. It ran the whole depth of the house from front to back and brought up against other fanlighted doors that led onto the back verandas. As they stepped inside, the cold air of the house closed about them heavily. A great crystal chandelier hung from chains above the staircase that swept up around it with living movement, the continual rhythm of perfect symmetry. Two great buffets stood on either side of the hall with portraits above them and great chairs flanking them, but the carpet between was a strip of worn straw matting. Double doors led off on either side and there were doors above on the gallery.

"In there," Buckmaster said, "is where my old woman found the burned shoes and the broken chair." Whether the silence of the house made his voice sound louder or whether some instinct made him speak more loudly because of the silence, Mat didn't know, but his hands twitched with the sudden sound.

He walked through into the dining-room. The fog glow through the east windows was obscene in that room. It was completely furnished but everything in it was ruined. The top of the long table was warped into rolling billows, and the satin of the chair seats hung from them like sunburn peel. The marquetry of the knife boxes on the buffet was sprung so badly that if you touched them or walked heavily across the rotting carpet, the boxes themselves would collapse. What a bloody crime to let a place like this rot out!

"There's the chair," Buckmaster said. It was propped on three legs against the wall, leaning there with a drunken leer, its broken leg lying rakishly across its seat. Mat walked over to the fireplace.

"I just shoveled everything out into the newspaper," Buckmaster said, "and took it into Mister Pyle."

Mat nodded. The open maw of the fireplace was directly behind the arm-chair at the head of the table—to warm the back of the Master of York. And on each side of it were great cupboard doors. Mat opened one to a winding flight of stairs and the rotting breath of the cellar came up to him. He opened the other door to a blank wall and cob-webbed ropes.

"Liquor," Buckmaster said.

"I get it—a dumb-waiter for wine."

"That's it, Mister Davanan. They'd keep a man down there during the dinner and send down notes for what wine they wanted."

"They certainly made the dumb-waiter big enough to bring up enough so they wouldn't run dry between trips." He reached into the cob-webbed ropes and gave a tug on one. There was a shower of dust and a hollow growl below and the dumb-waiter came up into full view. There was a wad of dusty cloth, a pair of shoes and a derby hat on one of the shelves. Mat reached for the hat and looked inside. It was a Borsolino hat purchased from Rogatti's in Turin and it bore the initials C.D.

"Say—" Buckmaster stared. "Them look like the striped pants your great-uncle was wearing the day he came over here!"

"I expect they are," Mat said. "Leave them here—for the police. Let's see the roof now." They went out into the great hall and up the stairs. At the top, Buckmaster opened a door to the left, off the gallery and led the way down a shuttered passage to a small powder room in the back of the house. He went ahead of Mat and opened another door. Narrow stairs led up behind it into the darkness above. Buckmaster started up, thrusting his great body in the narrow well and a moment or two later he was thumping heavily with his fist on something—it gave—and daylight flooded down the stairs. He had the roof hatch open. Mat climbed up and through it after him. Buckmaster had a crumpled cigarette package in his hand. Mat took it. "Fresh," he said, "with the New York City tax stamps on the cellophane."

From the roof you can normally see the whole spread of the York acres, the fields and the woods and the curving scimitar of Bligh River with that great fort of a boat-house that Charles Davanan built to take the *Paphos*. The west lawns, overgrown and scrabbled, led straight down to it in a gentle slope to the waters. But with the fog they could only see as far as a rough circular fence enclosing a depression in the ground and just beyond it, there were stakes around another depression with fence rails laid over them.

"Those are the cave-ins from the Captain's Run, aren't they?"

"They're cave-ins, no doubt—but I guess that Run's choked up. We had enough of it up here?"

"Yes—let's get after the boat-house now." Mat went down the stairs into the room below, leaving Buckmaster to close the roof trap. He walked out into the shuttered passage and through to the gallery. Just before he came to the door that led out into the gallery, he heard a door close on the floor below—a quick, decisive thump.

He went to the gallery rail and leaned over. Then he heard Buckmaster behind him and turned, and faced both barrels of the man's gun.

"For God's sake, Buckmaster—look out with that thing!" he sprang wildly aside, grabbing the gun-barrel with his left hand. Buckmaster's face was white.

"Did you see anything?" the man whispered.

"No—what should I see? I heard a door shut, that's all."

Buckmaster put the gun down slowly.

"I ain't never seen anything either," he breathed. "And I don't want to, I can tell you." There was sweat on his forehead.

"Come off it!" Mat said.

Buckmaster nodded without speaking. After a moment he said, "Yes, sir."

"More Dandy Davanan, I suppose?"

"Yes—sir."

"Rot!"

"Mister Davanan—if you're finished in the house, let's go." And he started down the stairs, carrying his gun. Mat followed him. On the landing below, Buckmaster turned and looked back. "Front door," he said, "breeze blew it shut. Gosh, I'm glad of that!" and he went on down.

Back at the truck Buckmaster said, "I kind of didn't want to go in that house to-day—even in daylight." He started the motor and drove on around the washing court and up an overgrown cinder road that led off into the fog. The house behind them faded into the fog. Mat said, "If you feel that way—maybe I'd better get somebody else to go to the boat-house with me."

Buckmaster said, "Mebbe you had, Mister Davanan. Mebbe you had." He seemed relieved somehow as if he'd set out to prove something and had proven it. He was almost cheerful.

As a New Yorker, Mat had a helpless feeling about rural policemen anywhere. It came over him now. This business needed a crack city man who could face the facts without local sentiment.

Suppose Buckmaster had had a hand with Innes in the killing of Charles Davanan and Tom Carter? The man was known locally as a competent farmer, dour but trustworthy. There was no evidence against him, only personal suspicion and until he had something more, he daren't, as a stranger, unload his suspicion in a community where Buckmaster was known. The authorities would only laugh at him to cover their astonishment—and that left Buckmaster still loose, but this time with a heavy grudge—a big rural screwball with a shotgun. No thanks. Not yet. Play it cozy. Buckmaster may have killed my uncle and Tom Carter to alleviate the boredom of a lifetime of listening to wheat grow, but if there was anything here at York that Innes wanted, he could have got it for him without murder. The furniture in the house? There's a lot of fine stuff there that could be fixed up for the antique market—perhaps even for museums—but that house could be gutted any dark night of every stick in it, and no murder required. The answer must be that he's not in with Innes.

They had been rolling slowly up an overgrown road beyond the washing court. Buckmaster stopped the truck.

"What now?"

"Cemetery," Buckmaster said and he went around to the tail gate and took out his pick and shovel.

"What for?"

"Mister Charles' grave," Buckmaster said quietly.

"What the hell do you mean, Mister Charles' grave?"

"Just that, Mister Davanan," and he stepped across toward the wall and legged over it, Mat after him. "Wait a minute, Buckmaster. What are you going to do to the grave?"

"See if Tom Carter's in it."

"Now hold on—you can't do that!"

"Why not? I buried Mister Charles—I can unbury him."

"Not without permission, you can't!"

"I sure can, if you say so. The burial ground is private. It's yours. I came up yesterday just before sundown when my old woman told me somebody'd been at that grave—and somebody had. If somebody killed Tom Carter what'd be more reasonable than to put his body in a brand-new grave? Ground's soft still and nobody likely to see the grave's been disturbed. And nobody ever likely to look."

Mat stared at the man. There was a coldblooded reason to him that was frightening. He stalked on through the tall grass around the serpentine brick wall of the burial ground without speaking again. He walked diagonally across toward some newer stones and put his gun against a truncated shaft of granite. He took off his bearskin coat and picked up the shovel. Mat just stood there and stared at him. Buckmaster cut the yellowing sods—the grass hadn't taken again at that time of year—where they had been cut before, and laid them back carefully. Then he started to dig into the earth below. There was something horrible in the way he went at it. It was a job to him, nothing more. He spat tobacco into his calloused hand and booted the shovel into the soft earth as if he were digging a trench. Mat lit a cigarette, fascinated, unable to keep his eyes off Buckmaster.

The quietude of the fog-bound morning lay over that acre of death like the silence that follows musketry fire—broken in thumping rhythm by the dry cough of the shovel hacking into earth. Mat stood still as long as he could, then he walked slowly down the overgrown gravel of a path, tugging at his cigarette, glancing casually at the stones.

TO THE MEMORY OF
Thomas H. Davanan,
ESQUIRE ATTORNEY AT LAW
WHO DEPARTED THIS LIFE 27TH OCTOBER, 1783, AGED
TWENTY-FOUR YEARS. HIS BENEVOLENT TEMPER, HIS AMI-
ABLE MANNERS, HIS TALENTS AND VIRTUES HAD ENDEARED
HIM TO A LARGE CIRCLE OF ACQUAINTANCES AND PROMISED
TO RENDER HIM AN ORNAMENT TO HIS PROFESSION AND TO
HIS COUNTRY. HIS PREMATURE DEATH REGRETTED BY ALL
IS PECULIARLY AFFLICTING TO HIS AFFECTIONATE RELA-
TIVES AND FRIENDS IN WHOSE HEARTS HIS MERIT IS MORE
INDELIBLY RECORDED THAN ON THIS PERISHABLE MARBLE.

And ten paces beyond that a flat piece of marble sunk into the
ground:

TO THE MEMORY OF
Captain the Honorable Eric Molleston
Royal Navy
DIED OCTOBER 20, 1809

Mat stopped in his tracks, staring at that tombstone and the
chill race came back to the nerves in his arms. For one awful
moment it was as if he had seen his own name there. He turned
his back on it abruptly.

Close to the cemetery wall he could hear Buckmaster's shovel
still coughing into the earth. Mat went back slowly down the
path to Charles Davanan's grave.

Buckmaster looked at him casually. "It's Tom Carter, all
right," he said.

"What's Tom Carter!" Mat stopped dead in his tracks,
looking at the man. There was a thin sweet horror in the air
now, weaving through it, spoiling it utterly, greening it almost

visibly. He looked down into the half-opened grave, holding his breath—and then he was sick to his stomach—quickly, impersonally, without knowing it was happening. And that was a fact, too.

"You had me fooled," Buckmaster grinned. "I thought you were the solid type nothing could get at. Nothing you could see."

CHAPTER FOURTEEN

M AT wiped his mouth with his handkerchief and threw it away, turning his back on the half-opened grave, holding his nose. "Cover it up, Buckmaster."

Buckmaster stepped over to him, closing his great fingers on his arm. "I tell you it's Tom Carter—just as I thought it would be yesterday when my old woman told me about the grave and the burned clothes—when I came up and saw them."

"All right—it's Tom Carter—but there it stays for the present."

"Somebody's killed him and put him in Mister Charles' grave. We got to take him to town to Dr. Sevenoaks."

"Not a chance," Mat said. "We may have had a right to open that grave, but we've got no right at law to touch the body now we've found it—until the law sees it first."

Buckmaster scratched the back of his head. "Just as you say, Mister Davanan."

"I say cover it up!"

"All right, but I brought Mister Charles in just like I found him," and Buckmaster walked back to the grave.

Mat turned and looked at him. My God, he looks like a murderer, he thought, and he certainly has an unerring sense of where the bodies are. He goes out duck shooting and finds my great-uncle and he comes up here with me and finds another gentleman who has departed this vale of tears somewhat abruptly and long enough to be noisomely unpleasant about it. Not only that, he finds 'em both—first crack out of the box. It wouldn't be logical that he knew where they were before he started out to find them, would it? He turned around and glanced at the shotgun. It stood beside Charles Davanan's grave, still propped against the truncated marble shaft. Mat put his hand in his jacket pocket and closed it over the .38 that was still wrapped in his handkerchief.

"Well, now what, Mister Davanan?"

"Now we go into town and get the police," Mat said.

He half turned toward Buckmaster with his hand on the gun in his pocket and he kept half-turned that way, no matter how Buckmaster moved, so that if it came to a quick shot, it'd be his shot first. Buckmaster put the pick and shovel across his shoulder and picked up the shotgun. He legged over the wall and Mat climbed it after him.

"There was a boat on the river last night—an oysterman."

Buckmaster spat heavily. "You sure?"

"Yes. The man in it anchored off the boathouse and when I hailed him he upped anchor and went on up the river."

"Well—there's Owen Twitmyer keeps a boat on his place up the creek. And two colored fellows named Tanner have an old motor dory. They live in Easting. And Blodgett Trippe's got an oysterman at his place and Dummy John lives on his in York Cove when he can get it to float. And he fishes when he can get it to go. Those are all the boats belong on the Bligh. You see it ain't rightly a river—it's this bay that makes in here from the Chesapeake behind Wreck Point—with the Creek emptying into it like."

"It must have been one of those four boats we saw last night."

"Yep. Musta been."

Mat stopped and looked down the slope toward the boathouse below on the river's edge, and then he walked down slowly toward the first cave-in of the Captain's Run.

"Don't go any nearer."

"Why not?"

"Ain't safe," Buckmaster said.

"Look, Buckmaster, if you draw a line between these two cave-ins," Mat pointed down the slope, "and continue it in a straight line toward the house and toward the boat-house—it leads to both of them. The book says one entrance to the Captain's Run was supposed to lead to the house. Why wouldn't the other be inside the boat-house?"

"Might be," Buckmaster said, "if there is a passage."

"Who put this fence up?" Mat stopped near it. The ground sloped bowl-shaped from the circular fence inward to a ragged tufted hole in the center.

"I put 'em up. This one about ten years ago, and the one yonder about three years ago when Mister Goldsboro was over to look at York."

"Did you ever go down the holes?"

"Why should I? I built the fences far enough back from 'em to get solid ground for the posts—but the ground's given since, you can see. My belief is they're old wells or cisterns."

Mat picked up a stone from the rank crab grass at his feet, aimed it underhand and chucked it over the fencing into the hole. It disappeared, but there was no sound of its striking below.

"Well—that's that." And they turned again and walked slowly back toward the truck.

Buckmaster threw his pick and shovel in back. "That all you want of me now, Mister Davanan?"

"Hell, no," Mat said. "You're coming into town to Chief Auls with me."

"Not before dinner I'm not. I'm hungry."

"I'll buy you dinner at the hotel."

"Not me," Buckmaster said. "I eat home."

Mat looked at him. "You better come in with me now," he said quietly. "We've got to tell 'em about Carter."

"Mister Davanan, you've got a right to ask me to do anything around here you've a mind to, but dinner time's my own time," and he climbed in and started the truck. "I'll run you out to

Thorpe's Corners for the noon bus from the ferry and you can go in on that. I'll meet you in town at Talbot Pyle's after dinner." That was that—definitely.

They got into the truck and Buckmaster ground it around on the overgrown cemetery road, headed it back and started for Thorpe's Corners. As they passed the box gardens, the fog had thickened so that they couldn't see the house walls. They got into the back road, tooled down through the break in the fence and wobbled slowly out into Wreck Point Road. Half way to Thorpe's Corners, a car, at the side of the road, loomed up ahead of them. Buckmaster slowed and drew in beside it. Broken tire.

"Need any help, Ned?"

"Hello, Miers—nope—got 'er almost fixed. Thanks. Nasty morning."

Mat saw the black and gold sign on the windshield: "Taxi."

"Look here, Buckmaster," he said quickly. "What's a taxi doing out here?"

"Say!" Buckmaster said. "That is kinda funny. Ned," he called, "what you out this way for—your health?"

"No," Ned shook his head. "Old fella at the hotel wanted to come out for some reason."

"Come out where?" Mat said.

"Had me drop him nearest walking distance to the old house at York—the Davanan place."

"Who was he?"

"Fella named Montgomery."

"How long ago?"

"About half an hour. I let him off at the back road. He walked in."

"How's he going to get back?"

"That ain't my business," Ned said. "He paid me for the trip. I got my own troubles," and he went on pumping his tire.

"O. K.," Buckmaster said. "Take it easy," and he started the truck again. "Kinda funny—anybody going to York a day like this."

Mat said, "You're damned right," and they drove on into Thorpe's Corners. Through the fog now you could just see both sides of the street—the post-office and Canby's Store, and on the steps of the store Old Andrew Goldsboro was sitting. He was like an apparition from the past—one of those benign little old ladies who sit in rocking-chairs in old houses—and are taken for granted by the people who see them, and raucously scoffed at by people who don't. For one awful second Mat knew that if he gave him the double-take, the old man would be gone, the steps empty.

Andrew Goldsboro's green umbrella was upright between his feet. He had clasped his gloved hands on top of it. He was buttoned tightly into a very old tweed ulster and his white side-whiskers overlapped the woolen scarf that was wound around his neck. He had old-fashioned canvas brief-case snugged under his left arm, and for this junket across the Bay and into the country, he had changed his silk hat to a gray, square-topped derby. He was wrapped heavily in ponderous Dickensian meditation. His old eyes were glazed with it—the world gone before it. But he was there, all right, in the flesh.

"Oh! Oh, yes. Good morning, Mr. Matthew." His voice was solid and comfortable. Nothing ruffled Old Andrew, neither time nor place nor people.

"I'm certainly glad to see *you*, sir," Mat said. "You got my telegram?"

"That is one of the reasons I am here," Andrew nodded. "Good morning, Buckmaster."

"Good morning, sir."

"I came up on the ferry bus," Old Andrew said. "Mr. Canby is trying to get you at the hotel now on the telephone, to have you come out and meet me. Buckmaster—suppose you go in and tell him Mr. Matthew is here."

Buckmaster clumped up the steps and into the store.

Mat said, "The whole thing has jelled—all we have to do now is get the police."

"Suppose you tell me."

Mat said, "Briefly this," and he brought him up to date.

"H'mmm." Old Andrew shook his head. "So Lord Innes is at York now—and that nice-looking girl isn't what she seems to be—and somebody tried to kill you last night at the hotel, and you and Buckmaster have just found this Government Fisheries man's body—and whoever broke in on Lord Innes in New York and said, 'No—not this time, I'm warning you,' also broke in on you in New York and that man is English Frankie Crimmins, according to the Federal Bureau of Investigation."

"Look," annoyance at the old man crowded in Mat's mind, "Nobody's broke in on Lord Innes. That was a cover up. He's English Frankie Crimmins himself and the girl's his accomplice."

"Is that thinking—or is it assumption, Mr. Matthew?"

Mat flushed.

"I have known your blood for seventy-odd years, Mr. Matthew," Old Andrew said. "There is much that I admire about it and much that I don't. Impatience in any one, I deplore, as an attorney-at-law. And as an attorney, I don't like clients to ignore my advice. By speeding everything up you have hindered my work. You should never have come down from New York without coming through Baltimore and seeing me first. Your haste hurried every one, including me, and I am an old man who detests speed."

Mat stood silently for a moment, held in his anger, then Old Andrew touched his hand. "You're not angry with me, my boy. You're rattled over finding this body, naturally—and you're angry at yourself. Why?"

"I suppose—because I was so completely taken in by the girl. She seemed so young—so decent—so—"

"Yes," Andrew nodded. "Tell me now about this Mrs. Vom Bloercke, please. She was at the hotel last night, too?"

Mat realized suddenly that he had been talking deliberately to Old Andrew about the girl, because he didn't want to talk to him or any one else about Mrs. Vom Bloercke. All morning, she had been heavily in the back of his mind, while he went on about this York Seat business. Heavily—but quite privately, his. Subconsciously, he wanted to keep her out of the whole thing— off the tongues of other people—entirely to himself. But suddenly as he looked at Old Andrew Goldsboro, he knew what his reason was. Shame.

He saw the realization of that shame in Old Andrew's eyes. Slowly, all of Mrs. Vom Bloercke was going to pieces, fading into the fog around him. She was plausible only when she was present before him to look at him, compel him with her voice. Away from him, none of her rang quite true—not nearly as true as Anne still rang, even though it was a fact that Anne was what she was.

"Yes," answered Mat, "Mrs. Vom Bloercke was at the hotel."

"Will you tell me more about her—can you?" Mat flushed slightly.

"She was at the hotel, she motored down from New York— started the day before we did—stayed at the hotel a few hours to rest and drove on south toward Salisbury."

"And you don't find that significant," Andrew Goldsboro said. "You find her merely a fascinating woman, and so you leased her York Seat."

"Certainly not. I indicated to de Wolff that I might in a few weeks. But I don't intend to lease York Seat to any one until I find out who committed the murders."

"And you made that quite plain to her and to de Wolff?"

"Of course."

Old Andrew sighed. "Growing old," he said, "is a most amazing process. One spends half one's life seeing things too close to one—so close that they confuse—and the other half seeing them so far away that one can not be a part of them. On the whole, I think I prefer age, however, for it releases one from distracting stimuli and allows one the fullest freedom of one's brain." He opened his brief-case and took out some papers and held them for a moment in his gloved hands. "Mr. Matthew," he said, "these," and he waved the papers, "would have brought me over—even if you hadn't telegraphed. I commend them to you. Read them." He sorted through them for a moment, then he held out a letter to Mat. It was on Sloan, Satterlee, Upjohn and Faynes' paper, 40 Wall Street, New York City, signed by Ralph Sturdevant Upjohn and inscribed to Mr. Andrew Goldsboro, Attorney-at-Law, 24 Ferris Street, Baltimore, Maryland:

DEAR SIR:

Your client, Mr. Matthew Lloyd Davanan has this day forwarded to me signed leases in favor of Mrs. Madeleine Bligh Vom Bloercke for his property of York Seat in Maryland, for a period of three months.

I have had Mrs. Vom Bloercke execute these leases and following instructions from your client, I forward his copy to you.

Yours very truly,

It was dated the day before Mat left New York.

"It's impossible," Mat said. "I sent him no leases and no instructions. Have you a copy of the lease?"

Andrew Goldsboro held it out to him, folded with the typed superscription up:

MATTHEW LLOYD DAVANAN
Landlord

To

(Mrs.)
MADELEINE BLIGH VOM BLOERCKE
Tenant

LEASE

PREMISES *York Seat, Maryland*
NO .... STREET .... CITY ....

TERM *3 months*
EXPIRES *December 18th*
RENT *$1,500.00*

Mat opened it quickly. It was a general printed lease form. It carried his own signature as landlord on the first page, with Madeleine Vom Bloercke's signature below it, both properly witnessed.

"But it isn't possible," Mat said. "Sloan, Satterlee, Upjohn and Faynes are a reputable firm. They're tops in New York and Ralph Sturdevant Upjohn is as well known in his way as Max Steuer."

"I happen to know that," Old Andrew nodded. "That is why I came over here to see you—not entirely because of your telegram."

"But I didn't sign this lease! It's a rank forgery."

Old Andrew nodded. "Upjohn has no way of knowing it, you see. He doesn't know you from Adam. Apparently he received them by mail."

"He took particular pains to assure me that Mrs. Vom Bloercke was a former client of his and that she was all right. He wrote me a letter. So did the president of her bank."

"Yes," Andrew said. "And I have no doubt that her check is good and that in certain ways she is all right." He smiled. "Nor have you, my boy, by the way you defend her."

"Don't be ridiculous! When a woman comes to you and introduces herself as plausibly as she did, and when her bank writes you, and her lawyer writes you, and her doctor makes a personal call on you—"

"You should—if you are experienced with women—become suspicious," Andrew smiled, "because it is a bit too good, isn't it? What I mean is that the more experienced a man is, the easier it is for a woman to talk him out of anything—without reinforcements."

Mat wasn't listening to the old fellow—his hand was on that thirty-eight in his pocket—cold against its coldness.

"But look here—"

"You still didn't sign it—is that what you are going to say?"

"Of course I didn't sign it!" Mat roared.

"But—" Andrew said, "if you had died last night in the Chincoteague Hotel—that would be very difficult to prove, wouldn't it?"

"Good Lord, sir!"

Andrew Goldsboro sat for a moment silent. "Timing," he said, "timing explains it. You offered to lease the place, but not at once. Mrs. Vom Bloercke had to have it at once—so she got it this way. You came down here too quickly—so you had to die. Your great-uncle came over here unexpectedly. He had to die—so did Carter—probably for just stumbling on whatever was going on."

"But where do Lord Innes and the girl fit in now?"

"I do not know. But I do know this—that they want York Seat, too—and that somebody in New York warned them against it. 'No—not this time. I warn you.' That man who broke in their hotel rooms."

"Check."

"And if it was the same man who broke in on you, what more likely than that he broke into your place to get a specimen signature to forge this lease from?"

"That's it—but I still don't understand—Mrs. Vom Bloercke's lawyer—her banker—her doctor—"

"This lease came to me from her lawyer in New York," Andrew said. "Ralph Sturtevant Upjohn. I have no doubt that whatever she is now—that her banker, her lawyer and her doctor know her only as a respectable person. Shall we be her first callers, Mr. Matthew, now that she has settled in the country?"

"What do you mean, sir?"

"On the ferry coming over from Annapolis," Andrew said, "there was a moving van and a small car with her servants—a maid, a butler and a cook."

"How do you know?"

"Quite simple," Andrew said. "The servants' car beat the bus I came on here. But the bus beat the moving van. When I got here in the bus, Mrs. Vom Bloercke was sitting in her car in front of the post-office. She spoke to the servants, took one of them in her car and drove off toward York. Neither the van nor the two cars has returned yet."

"But she can't get away with that—she—"

"She what?"

"Last night she wanted me to go back to New York—"

"Perhaps she thinks you have gone—"

"Perhaps—"

"Or perhaps," Old Andrew said, "she thinks you are dead. Perhaps she tried to get you to go back to New York—to save your life."

"Well—whatever it is—we've got them bottled up now," Mat said, "for this is the only road out."

Andrew nodded. "Unless they have a boat." There was the sound of a car motor up the road in the fog, from the direction of the town.

"Then the girl and Lord Innes," Mat said, "are after the same thing—whatever it is—but they've come out second best—"

"I don't know," Andrew shook his head. "I liked that girl—"

"But she's not what she claimed to be—she's a fugitive from justice—"

The car they had heard came into view and slowed to a roll. It was Tommy Powell's car and Anne was alone in it. Her shoulders twisted sharply as she reached for the brake. She opened the car door and got out, her slender legs flashing. She stood there for a moment looking at the post-office—stood there, slim in the morning light, patting down her hair under the scarf. For a moment she didn't see Mat coming toward her. When she did, she raised her hand to signal him:

"Mat!"

He kept on toward her, without answering.

"Mat!" she called.

He came up to her and stopped. Her hands were trembling and she couldn't speak for a moment.

"Have you seen Lord Innes?"

He looked at her and all the old nostalgia came back to him, clouded with his anger. That she should be so fresh and clean-looking—so definitely decent on the surface—

"No—but I know where he is if that'll do you any good. So do you."

"What's the matter with you?"

"Plenty. Go on about Lord Innes."

She put her hands together tightly.

"He's come out here—somewhere in a taxi—to find you!"

"I don't believe you," he said. "As simple as that. I've checked up on you and I've found out that everything you told me about yourself, is untrue. You never had a New York driver's license—there's nobody in *Who's Who in Art* named Langdon and the Metropolitan never heard of an artist of any note named Langdon."

All the color left her face and she stood there looking at him, her lips pursed tightly together.

"You fool—you utter idiot—none of that matters now. What matters is that Lord Innes wants to tell you about that man at the St. Daviston. He was at the Chincoteague Hotel again last night. Lord Innes saw him in the upper corridor. That man is why we are here in this country, you fool! Lord Innes tried to find you this morning to talk to you—he traced you to Talbot Pyle's office and then he hired a taxi and came out here after you. The clerk at the hotel told me—when I came down to breakfast. Look." She gave him a slip of paper.

On it was written:

MISS LANGDON:

Our visitor at the St. Daviston was here in the hotel last night. This is purely a personal matter between me and Mr. Davanan. I have gone to find him. Please remain at the hotel until I return.

INNES

Mat said, "All O.K. except that your name is Layton—not Langdon."

There were tears in her eyes now—tears of anger. She gripped the car door as if she would tear it loose. Andrew Goldsboro had stepped up beside them. He put his hand on the girl's arm.

"Tell us," the old man said with infinite gentleness.

She stood there for a moment, holding herself together with that queer dignity that was an integral part of everything she did. Then she said:

"Everything I ever told you about me was true, except my name. My name is Anne Layton—not Langdon." She was going back into something now that she didn't want to touch, but she had to, for some reason that was important to her. That was what he had first seen in her—a sort of desperate honesty, a desire to be what she seemed to be even when she had kissed him in the cab. And suddenly he wanted to reach out his hand and stop her. But he couldn't, for they were so far apart now.

"My father was Roger Layton and he was an artist. A great artist. Ask Dr. de Cordova at the Metropolitan," she said hotly. "And he will tell you how great an artist my father was."

She stopped for a moment and closed her eyes tightly. Then she went on speaking quickly. "Does the name of Tony Hutchinson mean anything to you?"

"He killed a girl out on Long Island about a year ago. A rich good-looking softie who'd read about playboys and wanted to be one. Killed himself, too, didn't he?"

"Three weeks afterward, in Montreal—when they arrested him."

"Go on."

"There was a photograph of another girl on his bureau at Easthampton," Anne said. "All the newspapers ran it as the mystery woman in the case. It was my picture."

Mat was angry suddenly—a coiling, futile anger that burned in his veins and in the pit of his stomach.

"You started young with the rich boys, didn't you?"

"I didn't start at all," she said. "I met him in the Branders Agency a few weeks before the murder. I was modeling. He got that picture from them. I was at his house the night he killed Margaret Mayhew. There was a party. Several people said I was there, but nobody remembered my name. I left before the murder, but nobody remembered that either. I saw it all in the papers the next morning—with my picture as the mystery woman. I went all to pieces—panic. I drew out all the money Father left me and went straight to Rockefeller Center and applied for a passport. You'd be surprised how easy it is to get one under another name, if you're dumb enough to try. My passport picture didn't look like the Branders Agency picture, and the girl I took to identify me didn't even notice that I was putting my name down as

Langdon instead of Layton. I got it and got out of the country. It's the truth, I tell you!" she said fiercely. "I went all to pieces at the time. All I could think of was being caught and arrested and questioned—with newspapers tearing my heart out—and my not knowing anything about the shooting to tell them. So I ran from it—and got away—with everything but my name. But it was worth it! It's hard enough for a girl to get along in the world without having a rotten run in the newspapers to fight against. If they'd found me before they caught up with Tony Hutchinson, I would never have lived it down!"

They were silent for a moment. Then Andrew said, "And now, Lord Innes, please."

"I don't know a thing about him, except that I put an ad in the paper in London for a job—that he hired me—and that he's a grand old person to work for—"

"But you do know that he doesn't want access to York Seat to look for the bones of Napoleon?"

"Only since that man broke in on us at the St. Daviston. That was when I first began to doubt him."

"And we're to believe that, too?" Mat said.

She stamped her foot. "You're to believe everything I've told you now—on my honor as a lady—" she said. "And if you're incapable of understanding that—you're to believe it because I've already been to the police station in town and they are following me out—and that means eventually I'll be sent back to New York—to face running away last year."

"But the British Consulate General never heard of Lord Innes!"

"They wouldn't—you idiot! He's an Irishman. He travels on an Irish passport. He has nothing to do with the English at all. He's rabid on the subject. He won't even have himself listed in English peerages! He enjoined Burke to omit his name and his family shortly after the Free State. It's one of the most famous civil actions of modern times. He loathes what he calls Ascendancy

Families and he loathes the sentimentality of your professional Irishman. He walks between the two extremes." She looked in her handbag for a moment and took out a little blue morocco memorandum book. She opened it to the back pages and handed it to Mat and Old Andrew.

"I copied that from an old Debrett on the ship when we docked, in case the ship's news men or any one else wanted it."

They read:

The Knight of the Reeks. Malcolm Charles Edward Montgomery, 7th Baron Innes of the Reeks, 12th Bart. of the Reeks, 21st Knt of the Reeks, of Galleon Regis, County Kerry, in Ireland, D.L., F.R.G.S., educated at Trinity College, Dublin. Capt. late Royal Iniskilling Fus., served in South Africa 1899-1900, present at Graspan, Spion Kop and Magersfontein. b. March 12, 1881, s. his brother as 7th Baron Innes, 12th Bart. of the Reeks and Galleon Regis, 21st Knt of the Reeks in 1908, m. 15th Sept. 1910 Lucy Mary Plunkett, second dau. of the 6th Earl of Lampet and has issue Sub-Lt. Charles Edward Montgomery, R.N. b. 16th Nov. 1911. Philip Montgomery b. 14 Sept. 1914.

Lineage: Sir Phillipe de Montgomerie d'Innes came to the country with William the Conqueror....

Mat skipped on through a Sheriff of Tipperary, a Colonel of Dillon's Regiment, an Admiral of the Blue, and a Brigadier on the Peninsula, and looked up at Anne.

She was holding back the tears of vexation nobly, her head high and her eyes very wide and bright.

He shook his head and grinned.

"No," he said, "no guillotine, Anne."

"Shut up!" She stamped her foot. "You're so smart—you think—"

"Anne—"

"Don't—"

Mat took the girl's wrist. "You damned little fool," he said, "to run away—to change your name!"

Buckmaster came out of Canby's Store.

"Chief Auls is on his way out here with Doc Sevenoaks and Talbot Pyle."

CHAPTER FIFTEEN

THE two cars from town, with Chief Auls in the first and Dr. Sevenoaks, the Medical Examiner, and Talbot Pyle in the second, drew up in front of Canby's Store and the three men got out.

"Morning, Mister Goldsboro," Pyle said.

"Good morning, Pyle."

"You must've driven out lickety-split, Miss," Auls said to Anne. "Danged if I could see in this fog. Morning, Mister Goldsboro."

Chief Auls was a very tall man, better than six-feet-six, with a badly slipped stomach that looked like a partly deflated basketball under his vest points which drooped with a heavily festooned gold chain that carried a carnelian seal and three gold rings with small green stones set in them. He shook hands diffidently with a red hand the size of a cut of beef, and his Adam's apple ran up and down his creased neck when he spoke, like a great bubble in a spirit level.

Dr. Sevenoaks was the local tribal medicine man of the County and he had no intentions of being mistaken for anything else. In his upper right-hand vest pocket he had a leather gadget that carried a fountain pen, a pencil and a thermometer in a case to match. His right-hand jacket pocket bulged with his stethoscope, the coiled rubber tubes of it plainly visible. At the lapel he wore a Red Cross button, but the final touch was his Van Dyke. It was combed neatly to a point and dyed jet black. His heavy eyebrows were iron gray and there wasn't a spear of hair on the rest of his head.

Chief Auls said, "Pleased," when he shook hands with Mat. Dr. Sevenoaks said, "Glad to meet up with you."

"This is awful," Pyle's fingers picked at his lips. "Buckmaster thought Carter was dead—this morning. His shoes are in my office. This is awful."

"There's a lot more than this Government Fisheries man to this situation," Old Andrew said, and he told them the whole thing from the start.

Dr. Sevenoaks toyed with the buttons of his overcoat. Auls pulled in his stomach with both hands. The heavy confraternity of officialdom settled down over the three of them. They were the Chief of Police, the State's Attorney, and the Medical Examiner of the County now. Their faces set into duty masks. These were the moments in life that those three men waited for. They had the solemn air of men sallying forth into the white light of public service. They nodded briefly as old Mr. Goldsboro brought out his points.

"Wait a minute," Auls said. "If this Mrs. Vom Bloercke is actually moving into the house now—she thinks Mr. Matthew Davanan here is dead—kilt last night in the hotel. For if she knew he was alive—she wouldn't dare exercise the fake lease."

"That's right," Andrew nodded. "She must think he's dead."

"Somebody's using her for a blind then—and selling her out by letting her go ahead and move in as planned."

Andrew nodded.

"Them servants that come over on the ferry—and the moving-van men," Auls said, "Two possibilities. They may be part of the gang—they may not. These servants, you say, sir—two women and a man. How many on the van?"

"Two."

"Three men then that we know about, and three women," Auls said. "We got six men and a girl."

Pyle coughed apologetically. "Possibly instead of just going to the house and pretending to call on this Mrs. Vom Bloercke—it might be more to the point if we went back to town and had Judge Twitmeyer give us a dispossess warrant."

Chief Auls said, "What good's a warrant, if you're dealing with a killer? Shotgun's the answer. I may not be a detective," he said, "but I know how to deal with a killer. So does Buckmaster. Him and me went through the Aisne-Marne and Soissons parties in France with the old Fourth Maryland. Buckmaster, do you solemnly swear to uphold the laws of this Town, County, and State of Maryland as temporary deputy sheriff without warrant?"

"I do," Buckmaster growled.

Chief Auls looked at Mat. "Do you, Mister Davanan?"

"I do."

"Pyle," Auls said, "we'll leave you out of any possible shootin' part." Pyle sighed in relief.

Auls looked at the doctor. "Do you, Doctor Sevenoaks?"

"I do."

Old Andrew Goldsboro stepped forward.

Auls looked at him. "Mister Goldsboro, perhaps you'd better stay—"

As Mat watched the old man he seemed to grow slightly taller. He was squaring his shoulders. "In the first place," he said quietly, "I feel that in my humble way I have worked this out to the point we have arrived at. I am an old man, but I have the right to see the last act. Swear me in, Auls."

"But—"

"Auls," Andrew smiled, "it's seventy-four years since I've heard a shot fired in anger, but to quote a United States Supreme Court Justice, 'when the fifes of yesteryear bleat in the brain, the laws of to-day fade.' I was at Deep Bottom, Virginia, with Longstreet, at Hatchet Run, and the long trek down to Appomattox with what was left of the Old Fourth Maryland in those days. I was a lieutenant of the line at fifteen. Swear me in, sir!"

"Do you," Auls gasped, "solemnly swear to uphold the laws of this Town, County, and State of Maryland as temporary deputy sheriff without warrant, sir?"

"I do. Are we ready, gentlemen?" Old Andrew picked up his tightly furled umbrella, just below the handle, and held it for a moment as if it were a blade. And in that moment, Mat saw what one sometimes sees in very old women at death—the momentous return of girlhood with all its fresh beauty—the fading of the burdensome years. Old Andrew was fifteen for a second, pink cheeked and keen of eye with a little gray forage cap pulled down frowningly to hide his youth—with sword in hand and his fresh boyish beliefs coiling in his mind. Almost, Mat could hear, "Steady men, steady the Fourth—" and then, "Come on! We've got the damned Yankees on the run. Yeeeow!" that long-dead Rebel yell.

Auls was looking at Old Andrew as if he saw the same things in his old eyes that Mat was seeing in his imagination. The last of an era—the last living flesh of a generation long since rigid in bronze and marble. A way of living and of thinking and of acting.

There was quiet respect in Auls' voice as he spoke to the old fellow.

"What are they after out there, Mister Goldsboro?"

"The old yacht in the boat-house," Andrew said.

"What's on it that they want?"

"None of you'll believe me if I tell you what I think," he said. "So I won't tell you, until I'm sure myself. Then I'll show you. Buckmaster, is the Captain's Run still open from the house to the boat-house, or is it choked up completely by cave-ins?"

Buckmaster looked at Pyle quickly. Pyle coughed.

"No, sir—it's open—all the way from the wine cellars to the boat-house," Buckmaster said. He turned to Mat. "I been trying to put you off that passageway and the boat-house but I ain't going to lie to you any more. You can do as you see fit, of course, but I'm as good a tenant as you'll get down here at York Seat. I got a still in the Run. Had it there most of prohibition. Still got it. Run off a couple hundred gallons of Maryland rye spring and fall. Ain't been to the boat-house since September."

Mat snorted. "Well, for Pete's sake, why didn't you tell me instead of putting on the act about the keys?"

"I didn't know how you'd take it," Buckmaster said. "Some folks don't understand those things. I was going to take the still down. It's like this: you'd understand it better if you lived here in the County. Even before Prohibition, we ain't had much truck with revenooers here. We made it right. Always have. It's a sight better than store whisky, ain't it, Chief?"

"I'll say," Auls chuckled. "A sight better."

"It's this way," Buckmaster said. "When the Federal men come over, they usually go to Mr. Pyle or Chief Auls here, to get the situation in the County from them. And they're honest with them. They just tip 'em off to the one or two rotten distillers—the ones that are always in trouble for other things, fellows who put lye in their mash—that sort of thing."

"That's right," Pyle said. "It's sort of understood, Mister Davanan. Of course, now that you own the place you can stop Buckmaster if you want to—but my advice is, you try his whisky first."

Mat looked at Pyle. "And that's why you tried to steer me off the boat-house, too, is it?"

"Well-a—" Pyle gulped.

Buckmaster said, "Look, Mister Davanan, Mister Pyle knows about the still, but he ain't in on it. I just keep him in whisky. I keep Chief Auls in it, too."

"It's all sort of understood," Pyle said. "I guess it's that way in most places."

Andrew Goldsboro laughed. "Do you make as good a whisky as your grandfather made?"

"Better, I guess—never drank his. But I've got a bang-up Gallislow still, Mister Goldsboro. Don't come any better."

"And that still is all there is behind all your mystery?" Mat asked him.

"Well, that's enough, ain't it, Mister Davanan?" Buckmaster said earnestly. "Enough to get clear of with all this other stuff going on. Now I got the keys to the boat-house right here in my jeans. Let Mister Goldsboro drive in the back road to the house—like they was calling on this Mrs. Vom Bloercke. Mister Goldsboro knows her and the lease has come to him. He can pretend he ain't seen Mister Matthew. Chief Auls and Mister Matthew and I can go to the boat-house by the Little Creek Road—go in it and come up to the wine cellars and into the house through the Captain's Run. That way we've got whoever's out there bottled up, we're bound to meet up with them somewhere before we meet up with each other again, and when we do—we got the mystery solved."

"Yep," Auls said and he walked back to the car. "Here you are, Doc—here, Pyle," and he handed them each a riot gun from the car. "Mister Goldsboro?"

Andrew lifted his umbrella. "This'll do," he said, "too old for shooting."

"You three get started then."

Sevenoaks climbed into his car. Pyle helped old Andrew in and the three of them started off.

Auls said, "I guess the girl better drive us. Can't leave a young lady standing in the road," and he grinned. Anne got into Tommy Powell's car and started the motor. Buckmaster, Auls and Mat climbed in the back. They rolled off into the fog toward Wreck Point—nobody speaking until suddenly as the girl turned the car into Little Creek Road, the silence got on Buckmaster's nerves.

"Strange thing at Mister Charles' funeral," Buckmaster shook his head. "He hadn't lived at York Seat for forty-odd years. Very few people even remembered him. Well, we was there in that empty house listening to the Reverend Moody read the service. Just Mister Pyle, Chief Auls, Doc Sevenoaks, and the Reverend Moody of Christ Church in town, and me and my missus. Funny about the missus—that was why she was the way she was this morning to you about living there—sort of gruff and unneighborly. My missus's always been jealous of York Seat. You got to know wimmen to understand it. Ain't one of 'em worth a damn if they grow up completely. That house is partly a doll's house to her—to play in—to play at cleaning up and keeping it looking like it ain't forsaken—and partly it's something else."

"What?"

"Well," Buckmaster pressed his lips together, "her great-grandmother was Sara Lloyd. The Lloyds married Davanans years ago," Buckmaster said. "Work's work to a man and what you do is what you are. But the missus, in her own mind, is a cut above tenant farming. Women can be like that. If it weren't for change, she might be a lady in that house. See?" Buckmaster went on. "Well—we was all there listening to the service and there came a knock on the door. My missus tells me to open it. Outside there was an old nigger named Bowlegs Phillipi, from Durburrow— that's the nigger village a mile beyond my house. Phillipi must be close to ninety. He was all dressed in his best clothes and there must've been a hundred niggers on the lawn of York behind him. Phillipi takes his hat off and he says, 'Mister Charles' servants are outside.' Well, you could've knocked me down—but there they were—all lined up in their best—people from Durburrow and Thorpe's Corners and Easting—men, women, and children."

"But I don't get it—what for?"

"To come to the funeral," Buckmaster said. "You see, Thorpe's Corners was always there, but Durburrow and Easting are villages that the Davanan people set up after the War."

"You mean slaves?"

"Yes, sir—and they never forget—the blacks. There ain't one of 'em around here'd set foot on York Seat for any other reason than a Davanan funeral but, by gum, every last one of 'em turned out for Mister Charles'. Mister Pyle let 'em in to walk past the coffin—and they was all there at the graveyard when we buried him. I can tell you, it was sort of uncanny."

The corners of Mat's eyes stung and he couldn't speak for a moment. With his imagination, he got it smack in the face. These colored people trudging in to York Seat behind old Phillipi, all dressed in their Sunday best to bury a Davanan they didn't know. Is that America—in this day and age? Good God, he thought, and I'm a smart guy who chases news and hangs from straps in the subway, and knows all the answers. But I've missed this cold, and it's been right here for me all along. 'Mister Charles' servants'— and again that impermanence of life came down over him—the sense of being himself only for his lifetime, of having a name and a life to move into and grace because it had been graced by other people of his name before him. And he found it infinitely better as a philosophy than the old free, white and twenty-one business with every boy an equal chance to be President. That made you scrabble like hell to prove yourself—for what? Your own ego in the final analysis. This other thing was beyond ego— ageless. And suddenly the Bligh woods were personally impor- tant. The problem of thinning them out, of draining more land for wheat. Of being a partner in Buckmaster's farm problems. After all, that's what the Davanans were—farmers. That's what all great families were—farmers. Lose the soil and you lose all. That goes for everybody from the Duke of Marlborough to Miers Buckmaster.

They were well beyond the Borghese Gates now and sud- denly, ahead through the fog, they saw a narrow leaden streak of water—the Bligh River. Anne stopped the car. Buckmaster and Pyle got out, Mat after them. They weren't two hundred feet from the boat-house. Buckmaster, shotgun in hand, strode toward the back door, tugging a bunch of keys from his pocket. Chief Auls was right behind him, his revolver out.

The blue fog hung in the trees like dusty surgical gauze. And the years were gone from the woods and the river and their age-lessness crept in. On just such a morning that long-dead raiding party from British boats in the Bligh River had crept up from the shore and taken slaves and the silver from the Davanans of York, before crossing the Chesapeake to burn Washington. These woods had been lighted by the fires of the Lenni Lenapes. They had echoed to the pistol shots of duelists and dropped back once more into the silence that held them now.

They kept on steadily to the boat-house, Buckmaster and Auls and Mat. Buckmaster put his key in the lock, turned it and pushed the door open with his shoulder. It was a moment before they realized that the front doors—the water doors—were open as well, that the pale opalescent light that flooded the shed came through them. Abe Laredo's *Paphos* filled the whole place, crowding them back, leering at them with the dead eyes of her portholes. She filled the whole boat-house, like a rotting corpse in its casket—a drowned corpse, swelling to burst what shreds of clothing still clung to it. The size of the yacht in that stone shed was frightening. She'd been hauled in by two great capstans and the cables that had hauled her in years ago still clung to her hawse holes, holding her with their rusted strength. The water that splashed was at the front end of the great stone shed—the rest of the slot was dry and littered with rubbish and balk ends around the heavy marine cradle that held her. Her rusted-out funnel with its guys swirling about it like tentacles lay on horses under her sharp bow and her cobwebbed masts were slung on iron brackets from the roof.

She was somewhere between a hundred-and-sixty and a hundred-and-eighty feet over all, that old boat of Abe Laredo's, with a jaunty clipper bow like a walking-stick in the hands of a ham actor, and a long overhang. A hell of a sea boat, as Andrew Goldsboro had said. But she didn't care now. She was alone with her memories, her deck-houses scabrous, her old hull furred with red rust. The great high bulk of her, brooding quietly on the beach forever, remembering, perhaps, the crowding bumboats of Mombassa, the gay lighted crescent of the harbor at Monte Carlo. Cowes during Cowes Week and the frightening winter splendor of the North Atlantic. Hungarian violins on the afterdeck and the laughter of Abe Laredo's many gallant ladies.

Time murders boats—time and not using them—and the *Paphos* had been murdered. She lay there in her cradle, inert, outraged, a lady in fashions that had gone hopelessly out of style.

They could see her boat ladder rigged as if she were lying at anchor, running down to the masonry floor of the boat-house.

Auls and Buckmaster started toward the ladder and suddenly Mat realized that Anne Layton was right beside him.

"Go back," he said.

"Judus Priest," Auls stopped dead and pointed. Against the wall of the boat-house, full in the light of the open water doors, lined up in a staring, arrogant row, there were six portraits. The damndest exhibit Mat had ever seen; they were all of the same man—or rather of the same face. It was a barber-shop face— puffy from hot towels and handling after an extremely bad night. It was small in the fat that held it, like a face molded in suet pudding, except the eyes. They had quiet power. Six of the most ridiculous portraits, all of the same man. He was in armor in one. In a sable surcoat with a golden chain around his neck. He was in a broad starched Flemish collar. He was on a chubby prancing sixteenth-century horse. He was staring at them arrogantly in a beautifully chased golden helmet. He was in knee breeches with white silk stockings, patent-leather slippers and the full face was a round, undistinguished moon, quite flabby but well cared for. Only the eyes had character. They were falcon eyes, powerful, but laughing at the ease with which they retained their power.

"Gentlemen! Right where you are, please!" and they saw the speed-boat in the water slot below, under the *Paphos'* counter, with Gabor de Wolff standing in it, holding a submachine-gun on them. "Drop your guns, please—at once!" he said and as he said it he started to do a most amazing thing as the shed filled with sudden horrid thunder. He started an adagio movement— he leaned sideways with a half-turn that threw one of his long legs over the other and the foot of it across the speed-boat's gunwale. He was in the air completely for a brief second, his mouth wide with surprise, his eyes staring at them—then he went loose all over, like a puppet when its threads are slacked, and he crashed downwards and lay quite still across the speedboat's engine housing—quite still except for the slight twitching of that one foot across the gunwale and the widening ripples below it where his submachine-gun had splashed into the water.

The thunder in the shed still echoed—the torn roar of a heavy calibered shot, and across the water slot they saw Lord Innes standing with a revolver in his hand, lowering its muzzle.

"Drop that gun!" Auls shouted.

"I don't think so," Innes said, "it's been with me since the Boer War." And he put it in his overcoat pocket. "I expect there will be slight complications about that shot—but remember, please, that he had a machine-gun trained on you when I fired." Lord Innes was standing very tall and very straight, buttoned tightly in his overcoat, his hat firmly on his head. His fine old face was quite beautiful in spite of the heavy fatigue that lined it. "Mr. Davanan," he bowed slightly, "I beg you to forgive my tres- pass, but it was the only choice I had when I couldn't find you."

The girl clutched Mat's arm tightly to keep him silent.

Innes said, "He was my son—Frank Crimmins—Dr. Gabor de Wolff. Whatever you choose to call him. He was born Charles Edward Montgomery. But he was lost from the beginning. Some people are like that, I'm afraid. He has been in jail most of his mature life. He escaped three years ago and I have had agencies on his trail ever since. But he was fiendishly clever. He was always just a step ahead of me—always so plausible to people. Is he quite dead, do you suppose?"

Auls and Buckmaster climbed down to the speed-boat, Anne and Mat went over to the old man.

"Yes, sir," Auls said.

"Good," Innes nodded. "I almost caught him when he was working this York Seat business at the Bibliothèque Imperiale in Marseilles with Mrs. Vom Bloercke. In New York, if I hadn't been ill, I would have got him when he broke in on me at the St. Daviston. He did that, you see, to be sure that it was I who was following him. You must understand that it was a family matter even in his mind. A matter of the succession. He has a younger brother. Last night he warned me again—at the Chincoteague Hotel—as he had in New York. I knew he was here before me then and that there was no chance of keeping you out of it, Mr. Davanan—of keeping myself just a casual visitor to York, interested in Napoleon's bones. So I followed you out here in a taxi, missed you, and," he nodded to his son's body, "went on about my business."

There was a movement at the upper end of the boat-house and suddenly Andrew Goldsboro and Sevenoaks with Mrs. Vom Bloercke between them, were coming down toward Lord Innes.

Andrew stopped, raised his umbrella and pointed at that amazing row of portraits. "Abe Laredo," he chuckled softly. "The colossal vanity of the man! Abe Laredo painted after the manner of Rubens—after the manner of Franz Hals—of Velasquez, of da Vinci, of Andrea del Sarto, of Rembrandt."

"Aren't they the damndest things you've ever seen, sir?"

"Are they, Mr. Davanan? Well, we'll see. Abe Laredo was a great character. There wasn't any business he didn't have a hand in—including art. He bought everything, and stole what he couldn't buy and carted them off. There is a list of five hundred paintings in the book that he owned at one time, some of the most famous paintings in the world among them. Abe was a pirate, and good pirates fly their jolly Rogers openly. He flew his, right in the face of the whole world. It is still flying for the world to see. I think these pictures are the monuments to Laredo's vanity—the one magnificent laugh he had at the world's expense. They hung openly in the saloon of the *Paphos* the last years of his life—he had paid for them to be stolen from the Naples Museum, Munich, the Chateau des Fimes, Paris, Budapest, and Willshire House—and he had his own face painted over each of the originals for the world to laugh uproariously at his bad taste, to overlook in its laughter the fact that he was a ruthless business man with infinitely good taste. A Franz Hals," Andrew said. "His 'Duke de Simmonetta.' Rubens's 'Burgomaster of Tache.' Velasquez's 'Don Jaime of Granada.' Andrea del Sarto's 'Knight of Turin.' Da Vinci's 'Il Moro.' And Rembrandt's 'Gentleman in Armor.' Better, I should say, than two million dollars in Government bonds, Mr. Davanan. When I gave up every other possible motive, I came to those six pictures that the inventory of the *Paphos* mentioned—and I had Abe's character from the book. I talked to Professor de Cordova in Baltimore a week ago, and he went through the Baltimore library. Those six pictures have been known to be missing for fifty years. I think we've found them."

"Pyle," Doc Sevenoaks said, "has the servants and the moving men lined up in the house for questioning. I guess somebody better get up there to relieve him. We brought the woman through the Captain's Run with us. She's a mite too clever for Pyle."

Chief Auls said, "Who is she?

Old Andrew looked at Mat. "You read the passages in *The Gay Laredo* that I marked—the passage concerning the Honorable Madeleine Forsythe's daughter who married Lord Astley-Thorndyke?"

"Yes, sir—but—"

"It is all a matter of going through with things, sir. When Lord Astley-Thorndyke divorced Madeleine Forsythe's daughter for presenting him, in turn, with an illegitimate daughter, he named Lord Challoner's heir as co-respondent and the divorce was granted."

"I read that—"

"I checked it by cable to London. Lord Challoner's heir was Herbert Bligh. Your charming Mrs. Vom Bloercke is Abe Laredo's granddaughter, Madeleine Bligh. Before she married Vom Bloercke she was a most successful actress on the London stage. It is just coincidence that her name is the same Bligh as we call the river after. Her New York lawyer knew her only through her divorce from Vom Bloercke in which she had the right, and her bank in New York, through the most generous settlement Vom Bloercke made her. I checked both sources by telegram."

Mrs. Vom Bloercke was standing there apart from the crowd. The light was in her hair and her baum marten coat was draped across her shoulders. All doubt—all confusion was gone from her eyes. As Mat looked at her he felt that strange compulsion that had come over him at their first meeting. There was no nonsense in his mind about Eric Molleston and Madeleine Bligh—but there was a feeling in him that he had known her much longer than he actually had. She did that to people. Frankness perhaps. Frankness that drew out frankness in him. An ease of manner that put people at ease.

She would speak in a moment and spoil the illusion utterly. He wished she wouldn't. This should end now—with no words, no parting. He was too tired for words—that fatigue that comes when one has been up since before dawn—a hot, sticky tiredness in the calves of the legs and the shoulders. He wanted to lie down for a few minutes and think this thing out quietly, but he knew as he stood there that it wouldn't think out. Every item of it went past reason, like floor boards in the darkness of an old house, then they cracked suddenly and sent you scurrying back.

Old Andrew blinked, still standing with his green umbrella and his brief-case hugged under his arm. Every nerve in Mat's body was drawn so tight that he couldn't have moved for a moment if he'd wanted to. But without moving he saw each face in that boat-house cut clearly. Anne Layton behind, her mouth half-open, utter disbelief in her eyes. Miers Buckmaster nodding in slow understanding. Chief Auls frowning heavily to cover the perennial good nature that he found a handicap in his profession.

Mat looked at Mrs. Vom Bloercke. Her face was drawn into hard lines and she looked desperately old and tired.

She said, "I would like you to remember that I did try to save your life—that murder is not in me."

"De Wolff murdered my great-uncle—"

"Yes," she nodded, "but I knew it last night for the first time. He told me. And he killed another man out here about a week ago. You see, he's been here most of the time for three weeks, searching for these things," she pointed to the pictures, "but I only knew last night that he had committed murder—that he would try to kill you—that's why I told you to go back to New York."

"Why didn't you tell me all of it?"

"I?" she said. "Why? I was definitely committed to it; I have found a record, too, and by staying with him"—she nodded toward de Wolff's body—"I have found the ultimate solution of life. Loyalty is a strange thing," she added, "but I have always believed in it. And this is how it ends." She shrugged. "At an old house on the Eastern Shore of Maryland. Ah, well, what is to be—is to be. And believe me, you must not think me blameless. I wouldn't have had my loyalty for him if it hadn't touched a chord in me.

"All my life I have lived by my wits. I am a thief, Mr. Davanan, as well as a good actress. Last night—on the hotel veranda," she smiled, "I told you the truth just before I left you. I tell you the truth now. Everything else was untrue. Good-by—but thank you for giving me one last decent impulse. I did tell you last night—to go back to New York."

Chief Auls took her arm. Buckmaster covered de Wolff's body and climbed up out of the speed-boat. Mat looked at Anne. Lord Innes stood just beyond them. He said:

"Those letters of Mrs. Henry Jerome's at the Bibliothèque Impériale—that is rather amusing, Mr. Davanan. Frankly, I used them merely as an approach to you. I had no faith in them. But would you mind—" he followed the others up toward the back of the boat-house and suddenly he lit a match—"I came down here, too—through the Captain's Run—following de Wolff, but apparently it branches into two passages that come to the boat-house—and I arrived by a different one than Mr. Goldsboro came in by. This is the one I came out of," and in the flare of the match he pointed to a tiny open door in the wall.

"Those letters of Mrs. Jerome's must have had some truth in them." He lit another match and held it up. "Or your ancestor, Mr. Robert Davanan, was a complete sentimentalist." The old man stepped down three steps. Anne and Mat followed him.

They were in a vaulted chamber. Lord Innes held his match high in the air. Above their heads, there was an archway with the keystone carved in alto relievo:

and just beyond it, a huge black basalt catafalque with that casket of red stone set upon it. A great bronze laurel wreath hung at the nearer end, with again the imperial cipher:

The back wall of the vault was a sheet of thick bronze with appliqued life-sized regimental flags of bronze on either side, and two lists of battles down the center:

Lodi	Austerlitz
Arcola	Jena
Rivoli	Eylau
Malta	Friedland
Pyramids	Wagram
Nile	Moscow
Jaffa	Lutzen
Marengo	Leipsic
Hohenlinden	Waterloo

"Sometime if you care to, I suggest you open his casket for medical examination of the remains. There are certain definite identifying marks mentioned in that dossier of letters of Mrs. Jerome, that should prove this assumption beyond a shadow of a doubt. And it is always amusing to confound the French—they take themselves so seriously."

He turned back to the steps and started up them again.

"Oh, yes, Mr. Davanan," he said softly. "My son's body. Will you allow it to be buried among the excellent company in your cemetery—when the police are finished? I shall leave funds at your disposal. After all, he was born a gentleman." He drew himself up and went slowly up the steps.

Mat turned to the girl. She covered her face with her hands and leaned against the wall, trembling violently. "Let's get out of this place, Mat."

"Not yet," he whispered. "Let him go up first. Steady—I'm that way, too. Here, hold on to me—complete jitters!"

She was crying then, but she looked at him, blubbering through her tears. He reached for her hand and held it tightly for a moment, then he pulled her toward him and she turned fiercely and clung to him, her body shaking with deep sobs.

"I didn't know," she said, "I didn't—How utterly awful."

"Steady, Anne—we've got it all now." And after a moment she wiped her eyes with his handkerchief and they went up the steps.

A faint sun spread across the tops of the fog as they came out of the boat-house again. They stood for a moment at the doorway. Old country haunted with the memory of old people. Safe country—for everything that can ever happen has happened there before. Laughter and tears, hatred and love and death, murder and childbirth and death in bed.

Anne's body stopped trembling under Mat's arm. Good Lord, he thought, this girl? Is it this girl? It must be. But for a brief second the memory of Mrs. Vom Bloercke crossed his mind. What was it she did to me? Something quite awful, if you analyze it, something desperately ecstatic, but not quite—clean.

"Anne," he whispered humbly, "forgive me."

And right beside them suddenly there was Old Andrew Goldsboro with his umbrella. He chuckled slightly as he started to walk along with them.

"There was a man here a moment ago, while you were inside with Lord Innes," he said, "but I didn't think you wanted to see him to-night, Mr. Matthew."

"A man—who?"

"His name was Croler," Old Andrew said. "He represents N. Haugwitz in Baltimore. The Baltimore Scrap Iron Company. I think you said you got a letter from them a while back. I told him to see you to-morrow at the hotel. He wants to buy an old steam yacht you have on your place. Don't sell it to him, he'll only break it up and send it to Japan for munitions. It deserves a better fate." Old Andrew chuckled. "Well," he said, "it's amazing how the mind lives on when the body gets almost too old, to hold it, isn't it, Mr. Davanan? If I'd had a few more days, I'd have worked this all out without stirring from my office. The book told the whole story. All any of us had to do was to read the book—to find out everything, but the ending—"

"I don't—"

"Oh, but you do," Old Andrew said. "Doesn't he, Miss Layton?" Old Andrew chuckled again. "We shall have champagne to-night, taken in broken glass, to the latest Davanan of York—a helpless tribe but amusing, my two young friends, I can assure you. I wish I'd known them all, but I'm quite old enough as it is, thank you. Filthy old. But life is still pleasant—still pleasant."

(1)